THE R

ANDREW SINCLAIR was born in Oxfc
and Trinity College, Cambridge. Al
History, he initially pursued an academic career in the United States and
England. His first two novels, written while he was still at Cambridge,
were both published in 1959: *The Breaking of Bumbo* (based on his own
experience in the Coldstream Guards, and later adapted for a 1970 film
written and directed by Sinclair) and *My Friend Judas*. Other early novels
included *The Project* (1960), *The Hallelujah Bum* (1963), and *The Raker*
(1964). Sinclair's best-known novel, *Gog* (1967), a highly imaginative, pica-
resque account of the adventures of a seven-foot-tall man who washes
ashore on the Scottish coast, naked and suffering from amnesia, has
been named one of the top 100 modern fantasy novels. As the first in the
'Albion Triptych', it was followed by *Magog* (1972) and *King Ludd* (1988).

Sinclair's varied and prolific career has also included work in film
and a large output of nonfiction. As a director, Sinclair is best known for
Under Milk Wood (1972), adapted from a Dylan Thomas play and starring
Richard Burton and Elizabeth Taylor. His nonfiction includes works on
American history (including *The Better Half*, winner of the 1967 Somerset
Maugham Award), as well as books on Dylan Thomas, Jack London, John
Ford, and Che Guevara.

Sinclair was elected a Fellow of the Royal Society of Literature in 1972.
He lives in London.

DR ROB SPENCE is a senior lecturer in English Literature and associate
head of department at Edge Hill University, Ormskirk. His main research
and teaching focus is on the modern and contemporary periods. He is the
author of a number of book chapters on Anthony Burgess, the subject
of a forthcoming monograph, and has written *A Student Guide to Louis de
Bernières*.

By Andrew Sinclair

FICTION
My Friend Judas (1959)
The Breaking of Bumbo (1959)
The Project (1960)
The Hallelujah Bum (1963)
The Raker (1964)*
Gog (1967)
Magog (1972)
The Surrey Cat (1976)
A Patriot for Hire (1978)
The Facts in the Case of E. A. Poe (1979)*
Beau Bumbo (1985)
King Ludd (1988)
The Far Corners of the Earth (1991)
The Strength of the Hills (1992)
Blood & Kin: An Empire Saga (2001)

SELECTED NONFICTION
Prohibition: The Era of Excess (1962)
The Better Half: The Emancipation of the American Woman (1965)
Guevara (1970)
Dylan Thomas: Poet of His People (1975)
Jack: A Biography of Jack London (1977)
John Ford: A Biography (1979)
Sir Walter Raleigh and the Age of Discovery (1984)
The Sword and the Grail (1992)
Francis Bacon: His Life and Violent Times (1993)
The Discovery of the Grail (1998)
Death by Fame: A Life of Elisabeth, Empress of Austria (1999)
The Secret Scroll (2001)
An Anatomy of Terror: A History of Terrorism (2004)
Rosslyn (2005)

SCREENPLAYS
Before Winter Comes (1969)
The Breaking of Bumbo (1970)
Under Milk Wood (1972)
Blue Blood (1974)

* Published by Valancourt Books

ANDREW SINCLAIR

THE RAKER

With a new introduction by

ROB SPENCE

VALANCOURT BOOKS

Richmond, Virginia

2014

The Raker by Andrew Sinclair
First published London: Jonathan Cape, 1964
First Valancourt Books edition, January 2014

Published by Valancourt Books, Richmond, Virginia
Publisher & Editor: James D. Jenkins
20th Century Series Editor: Simon Stern, University of Toronto
http://www.valancourtbooks.com

ISBN 978-1-939140-75-3
Also available as an electronic book.

All Valancourt Books publications are printed on acid free
paper that meets all ANSI standards for archival quality paper.

Cover by M. S. Corley
Set in Dante MT 11/13.2

INTRODUCTION

ANDREW SINCLAIR is a genuine man of letters, of a type that is increasingly rare these days. His privileged background (Eton and Cambridge) led to a varied career encompassing film-making (he directed Peter O'Toole, Richard Burton and Elizabeth Taylor in the classic film of Dylan Thomas's *Under Milk Wood*), biographies, social histories, and an impressively diverse series of novels. He did his National Service as an Ensign in the Coldstream Guards from 1953-55, an experience that provided him with the material for his darkly comic novel, *The Breaking of Bumbo*, which featured the first in a long line of misfit male protagonists in his work. In his later fiction, Sinclair increasingly turned to myth and legend, most notably in the three linked novels *Gog* (1967), *Magog* (1972) and *King Ludd* (1988), collectively known as 'The Albion Triptych'. A Fellow in American Studies of five universities, Cambridge and Harvard, Columbia and Stanford and University College London, he has produced major accounts of Jack London and John Ford and even Che Guevara. His work frequently blurs the lines between fact, fiction, and analysis, perhaps most spectacularly in *The Facts in the Case of E. A. Poe* (1979).

The Raker is Sinclair's fifth novel, and offers on one level a realistic account of the life of Adam Quince, newspaper obituarist at an unnamed London daily, but on another, a phantasmagoric, gothic vision of a city of death, inhabited not just by those caught up in the drudgery of modern urban life, but by the ghosts of their predecessors. Quince's life of tedium, partially relieved only by the bullying of his boss Noyes and the embraces of his ageing mistress Lottie, is measured out by the index cards of the dead and the dying which he monitors in his basement office 'morgue'. Sinclair evokes the cynicism and brutality of newspaper life by demonstrating how an obituary submitted by the friend of a controversial political activist is rewritten by Quince and Noyes until the bland platitudes of the original are transformed into a damning *ad hominem* attack.

What takes Quince's life into another dimension is his chance

encounter with the enigmatic John Purefoy, whose obsession with
death and its representation is overwhelming. The two become en-
gaged in a tug-of-war over an actress, Nada Templeton, with whom
Quince becomes obsessed. She is near death when she is intro-
duced, a condition that excites Purefoy and simultaneously repels
and attracts Quince. Purefoy is 'The Raker', named after the men
charged with keeping the streets clean during the plague epidemic
in London in 1665. Purefoy explains the nickname by quoting by
heart a passage from Defoe's *Journal of the Plague Year*, where the
author himself cites the ordinance of the Mayor for the mainte-
nance of cleanliness in the streets: 'That the sweeping and filth of
houses be daily carried away by the rakers, and that the raker shall
give notice of his coming by the blowing of a horn, as hitherto
hath been done.' Interestingly, this is the only reference in Defoe's
work to the raker, so Purefoy has taken on the mantle of an insignificant figure, in keeping with his nihilistic philosophy. Indeed,
Purefoy's maddening impulse to erase himself from life appears,
paradoxically, to be his *raison d'être*.

Sinclair's prose style reflects the two levels of the narrative. In
the realistic descriptions of London streets, dingy bedsits, hospital
waiting rooms and smoky offices, a naturalistic mode predomi-
nates, though always with some oddly disturbing detail: for in-
stance, the opening of the novel features a Fleet Street accident in
which, bizarrely, a badger is run over. Later in the novel, as Quince's
life begins to disintegrate, his drunken ramble across the city is
dramatised by Sinclair in a wild free indirect style that anticipates
his later experimental writing in *Gog* and *Magog*. It is here too that
the weight of London's history, with its countless dead, weighs
unbearably on the man whose business is the recording of death.
In an extraordinary stream-of-consciousness passage, Sinclair over-
lays the modern urban scene with the ghosts of London's history:

> The graves are opening. Opening the plague pits. Giving up
> their long-dead. Giving up the rotted, the sore, the wasted.
> All the rooms of the city are cemeteries. Giving up their
> long-dead. The badger is walking, down the Fleet river. The
> dead press about him. Rise, Adam, rise now. Till London is
> a street map, a forest, an estuary. In the black gaps of streets

or sewers or rivers or ditches, the dead pack and scrape each other. And who, who the dead of London?

As the novel reaches its grotesque climax, Quince's disorientation leads him to a final confrontation with the Raker, from which only one of them can emerge.

The Raker is at once a period piece, firmly set in the concretely described London of the early sixties, yet also strangely timeless, with its echoes of the seventeenth century, and its presentation of the flamboyant Purefoy, who seems to transcend period, but who has the style of a Wildean aesthete. The novel shows Sinclair at his most engaging, in a narrative which is as entertaining as it is disturbing.

ROB SPENCE
Edge Hill University

September 2, 2013

THE RAKER

To D. L.

PART ONE

The Last Gentleman

Because I could not stop for death
He kindly stopped for me
The carriage held but just ourselves
And immortality

We slowly drove, he knew no haste
And I had put away
My labour, and my leisure too
For his civility

EMILY DICKINSON

I

As Adam Quince approached the newspaper building where he worked, a news item took place under the windows of Fleet Street. A badger appeared from nowhere, and was run over by a double-decker bus. Adam saw the black-and-white creature dead in the roadway, while the driver of the bus and some passers-by looked curiously down. He crossed the street to join in the conversation of the mourners.

'What is it? A dog gone wrong?'

'A badger.'

'A badger in Fleet Street? Is this a record?'

'It must have come from the Zoo.'

'Perhaps it came out of a drain. The old Fleet river does run underneath.'

'The Fleet's a sewer now.'

'Badgers like dirt.'

'Not dirt that powerful. Perhaps a joker let it loose.'

'You never know what the papers won't do for news.'

Adam stared at the crushed snout and the striped flanks of the beast. Only the seeping blood was alive on its still length. As it lay there, it looked strangely relevant. Its colouring belonged to a city of concrete and tarmac. Adam remembered his old history column in the newspaper. For a year, he had been forced to read up on his adopted city. When York had been civilized, London was a mere swamp. Badgers had hunted in the marshes here a thousand years ago. The present streets were laid over their earths. Perhaps the instinct of brutes, like humans, was a quest for their roots.

As Adam crossed the road again towards the entrance to his office, he noticed another unusual thing. A vendor had dared to come into Fleet Street. This man was dressed in a dark suit and a bowler hat. His face was as fleshed and ruddy as any City business man. Only his open brown suitcase gave away his trade. That, and the specimen toys that stood at his feet.

The toys were some three inches high. They were replicas of

their master, with bowler hats and dark suits and red faces. They worked off a bulb held in his hand. When he pressed the bulb, which he did every ten seconds, the little men all raised their hats at once. When the spurt of air gave out, they lowered their hats again.

'I'll have one,' Adam said.

The man bent down and gave Adam a manikin in its plastic wrapper.

'Only two-and-six, sir.'

Adam paid and took the toy. As he walked off, he saw the vendor raise his own bowler hat in thanks. At the same time, the little men all raised their hats. Adam looked down at the legend on the plastic wrapper. Mr Good Morning says, Courtesy Counts.

Adam went in through the revolving door of the newspaper building, across the black marble hall, past the reception desk, and over to the lift. It was waiting for him. He entered. He was depressed each time that he had to touch the button to descend to the basement. No man should have to descend to do his work.

There was a note from Noyes, the news editor, waiting for Adam on his desk.

Comachin is dead. So will you be, unless the Chief gets three paragraphs on him in line with our policy. De mortuis nil nisi bunkum.

Adam looked forwards at the rows of steel filing cabinets facing him. They were painted green, and numbered carefully, a–am, an–be, bh–cj . . . Onwards to the end, z–zero.

The drawers of the files were piled vertical to the white ceiling, and horizontal round three sides of the square room. No windows anywhere, only the four blades of a black fan behind iron mesh. Behind Adam's desk, a door offered escape or entrance. On the small section of the fourth grey wall, a Van Gogh print hung. It showed a table and bottle and bread and apples, a still life.

Much as Adam disliked his office in the Morgue, he felt at home there. In his chosen separation of himself from his previous homes, his place of work had come to be the constant element in his life. If he felt superior to his surroundings there, at least he knew them. He had schooled himself never to betray his Manchester slum background and the gutter memories of his childhood. His speech denied slurred vowels with such precision that he might have spent years as an officer in the Army. He clipped his words into trim noises.

He was ridding himself of his suburban wife and child with less ease. When he had married, he had thought that he was doing better for himself; but this was only because he had not yet learnt that he could expect the best. For the Manchester youth, it was enough to find a job and a pretty wife in London. But for the London journalist, a rich mistress and the envy of the Fleet Street pubs was the just reward of charm and success. There was something in Adam's curls and red mouth under a straight nose that made people want to know him, briefly at least. His brown eyes were naturally warm, even in his indifference; and his body was easy under his clothes, or out of them.

He had left his married home at Purley, while his divorce was going through and making him poor. He was now living, as he had lived for the past eighteen months, in a room in another journalist's flat. He always stayed until his host's patience ran out, before he could bring himself to endure a bachelor's bed-sitting room at five pounds a week and the necessary hunt for other free resting-places. Adam never wondered why people invited him to call, and rarely to remain. He was proud of his own restless and vagabond spirit. At times, he referred to himself as a Bohemian at heart.

He had that quick willingness that does not ripen into forethought. He was eager to learn and judge, always in search of the right catchword to make himself leader of the pack. He believed that he could live and hunt alone; but he had never tried. Once, at the age of nine years, he had felt the horror of isolation, when his mother had awoken screaming in the night with acute appendicitis and had been driven off to hospital with his father at her side – perhaps to die – but then Adam had run out into the street, wailing, until the neighbours had taken him in. Since that time, he had thought that all talk of the unknown or the unpleasant was either pretentious or morbid. Adam wanted to live in the day, and he was pretty successful.

He rose to his feet and walked round his desk. He stopped in front of the files on his right. His left hand skipped down the handles, BH–CJ, CL–COT . . . The hand paused, gripped, pulled. The drawer slid easily out of the cabinet. The hand riffed along the cards within. *Colpit, Colpoys, Columbus, Colville, Colwell.* A finger made a dent in the cards, forcing the front cards to fall forwards on a slant. The cards were then flicked over one by one, with their brown envelopes following their descent. *Colwell, Anthony Jennings, Capt.* . . . *Colyer, Dame Elizabeth,* . . . *Comac, Ignatius,* F.R.I.C.S. . . . *Comachin, Peter* . . . Adam lifted up the envelope behind the card, brought it clear of the cabinet, and shut the drawer with his free hand.

The envelope on Comachin was bulging. He must have had a full life, or, at least, a notorious one. Adam returned to his desk and spread out the clippings from the envelope in front of himself. He began to examine and judge the evidence.

The Comachin story was a story of his time. Peter Grybalowski seemed to have been involved in every skirmish of the century. He had survived the First World War, although he had been drafted by mistake at fourteen years of age as a Jew into the Austrian army on the Russian front. He had taken the name Comachin when he joined the Communist Party in the 'twenties. He had fought against Hitler in Germany and against Franco in Catalonia. He had left the Communist Party after the Spanish Civil War, and he had fled to England on the fall of France.

Somehow, Comachin had managed to enlist in the British army, and had fought in North Africa and Italy. After the Second World War, he had become a competent novelist, a naturalized British citizen, and a propagandist for lost causes. He had last merited clippings for his work on the Committee of One Hundred. Old age had turned him into a pacifist. And death respected him enough to take him sleeping, offering no resistance.

His enclosed obituary had been written by a distinguished Socialist friend. It read:

> Peter Comachin fought for his beliefs all his life. His courage was his greatest quality. And yet, in the hour of danger, one remembered his humour. On the worst night of the blitz, he insisted on walking out into the burning streets with a diplomat from the Foreign Office, who was naturally reluc-

tant to go with him. 'I quite understand you,' Peter said. 'I do not have the sort of reputation a diplomat can be caught dead with.'

He was a lover of peace from birth. Although he warred against fascism and totalitarianism all his life, he was reluctant to take up arms. In the end, he thought that he had been mistaken in fighting at all.

He adopted the creed of passive resistance and world disarmament. He sat down in Trafalgar Square recently as he had stood in the Catalan trenches. He would always act bravely for his faith.

Wherever Peter Comachin moved with his fire and sincerity, he made many friends. He was a loyal and a generous man. If he had faults, they were the faults of too large a heart. There is a time for weeping now. We shall not see his like again.

Adam sighed. It was never safe to trust an obituary with a political slant to a friend blinded by the same ideology. A similar point of view made correspondents soft-headed. A man was not known by his fellow travellers, but by the ticket-collector. Adam turned to his typewriter and set about the work of correction, typing directly from the previous appreciation. The truth about Peter Comachin was buried there; it merely needed a little spadework. The new obituary took Adam ten hard minutes of honest toil.

Peter Comachin fought for his beliefs all his life, although at different times he was a Communist, a democrat, a revolutionary killer, and a pacifist. He had the courage of changing his mind. He was sometimes reckless. On the worst night of the blitz, he insisted on walking out into the burning streets with a respected diplomat from the Foreign Office, who was naturally reluctant to go with him. 'I quite understand you,' Comachin confessed. 'I do not have the sort of reputation a diplomat can be caught dead with.'

He was a lover of revolution from birth. He was against law and order all his life, and took every opportunity to fight. In the end, he changed his opinions with the latest fashion.

He adopted the so-called creed of passive resistance. He sat down in Trafalgar Square recently as he had fought against Britain's allies in the First World War, ready to heed the first call to arm against friend and to disarm against foe.

Wherever Peter Comachin moved with his fire and fury, he was deported. Except from this country, famous for its tolerance. We have taken in the Comachins of the world for too long. There is a time for closing the gates now. We do not want to see his like again.

When he had finished his remoulding of Comachin's life, Adam put his feet on his desk and lit a cigarette. He was angry that Noyes should come in on one of his rare visits, to find him horizontal.

'Only when the time comes,' Noyes said, 'will you put yourself in a position to be carried out feet first.'

Adam brought his legs back under the desk and handed Noyes the Comachin piece.

'All sewn up and ready to roll.'

As Noyes put the obituary near his left eye, Adam looked at his tormentor's face. He knew it so well. The thin hair licked into black tongues against the pink scalp. The one red, half-closed, genuine eye, and the one wide, blue glass eye. The lines that marked experience or bitterness or loose skin. The cigarette scum on the corner of the mouth that even Noyes's frequent cough could not blow away. And the dandy folly of the fresh carnation in the lapel of the worn suit, the last wag of youth from an old dog.

And yet, when Adam was drunk enough to tell the truth to himself, he could admit that he had admired and copied and lost to Noyes ever since he had joined the newspaper. Fundamentally, he believed in Noyes, although he was sure that he only believed in himself. And, in his turn, Noyes was flattered by Adam's faithful imitation. He felt himself most perfect when he saw his flawed image reproduced by his follower. If Noyes was the man Adam would like to have become, Adam was the man Noyes was glad to have outgrown.

In a newspaper where the rate of sacking was higher then the life-expectancy of a second lieutenant in the First World War – one removal for every ten days – Noyes had survived in the front line for twenty years. He had reached the news editor's desk, and had even persuaded his employer that he was indispensable. 'Indispensability,' Noyes had once defined, 'is the power of making fools believe your ghost walks in the office when you're dead drunk in the pub.'

Noyes read through the obituary with a professional's speed.

'It's got the meat,' he said. 'But where's the pep?'

'I thought it was a think piece.'

'We'll up it to editorial matter. Which makes it fool's gold. Where's the original?'

Noyes also read through the Socialist's appreciation of his friend Comachin. He laughed.

'Do you trust yourself, Quince, enough to walk towards the sun? Your own shadow might stab you in the back.'

'I never see the sun down here.'

'That's to save you from yourself. Quince, do you really believe in the Chief?'

Noyes's glass eye reflected the light of Adam's desk lamp in a prism of glare.

'I believe in him,' Adam said.

'All the commandments of the Chief?'

'Most of them.'

'Including, Thou shalt not bear false witness, except if the Chief says it's true?'

'He pays me, doesn't he?'

'Yes, Quince. But how do you know that the Chief exists?'

'He lives in Bermuda. He talks on the transatlantic blower every day, sometimes even to you. I've read all about him and his palace and his handmaidens a thousand times.'

'Where have you read it?'

'In the papers.'

'But people like you write the papers. Can you believe them?'

'Yes,' Adam said. 'They get the essentials.'

'Supposing I told you,' Noyes said, 'that the Chief had been dead for several years.'

'No.'

'Yes. He spent his old age dictating general policy on to endless tapes, which were to be played daily for the next century. On his death, he was embalmed and set up in his wheel chair. Each day, his faithful secretary plays a posthumous tape to the London office. And in Bermuda, the Chief sits there, nodding wisely by means of a small balancing mechanism sunk into his neck.'

Here Noyes paused and picked up the manikin which Adam had bought that morning. He stripped off its plastic wrapper, stood it on the surface of the desk and pressed its bulb. The manikin raised its hat politely.

'By means of bulbs held in the secretary's hand,' Noyes continued, 'the Chief can receive visitors. He takes off his famous cricket cap to ladies. He nods to gentlemen. He can also, it is said, drop his lower lip sufficiently so that a cigar can be pushed between his teeth and lit. Then he listens to fraternal greetings, preserves the silence of the wise and finally says, "Thank you, dear friends" – note the sexless farewell – from a microphone hidden under the fresh rose in his buttonhole. The visitors go. Outside, they talk of the brilliance of the Chief's mind at the age of ninety. All the funny stories of the time are attributed to the old lion. As he gradually decomposes, so his reputation grows as sage and wit. The Chief is dead, Quince. Long live the Chief!'

'You're joking, Noyes.'

'Am I? Have you ever seen the Chief?'

'No. Never.'

'Isn't he the only Being you accept on faith alone?' Noyes asked.

'I suppose so.'

'Who has seen him over here for several years?'

'No one on the paper.'

'We hear his voice. But many heretics have been burned at inquisitions, my dear Quince, for claiming that they are guided by heavenly voices.'

'He couldn't have planned to live like this after his death.'

'Why not? Resurrection is always possible through memoirs or a faithful secretary. The evil that men do lives after them, Quince. That is what last wills and testaments are for. The good is oft interred with their bones. Not in the case of the Chief, because he is still unburied, and there was no good in him ever. He just sits over there, a mouthing mummy as he's always been, wrapped in a shroud of red, white and blue, preserving posterity from looking after itself. On him, the sun of empire never sets, mainly because it's been painted in a patriotic mural on the ceiling. Praise ye the Chief! O come let us adore him!'

'I'll hire you a pulpit, Noyes.'

'I sit in one already. You may think my seat is only at a desk. In fact, it's at an altar. I tell you about the Chief's wishes, don't I, Quince?'

'Yes.'

'You accept what I say. For the Chief to you is unknowable, invisible, omnipotent.'

'He's in Bermuda.'

'What's Bermuda to you? The Isle of the Blessed? Atlantis? Paradise? You'll never get there, Quince, until you're dead to us.'

Noyes pressed the bulb of the manikin again. It raised its hat.

'Who's on the end of your bulb, Quince? Me. And who's on the end of my bulb? The Chief, who I've never met, and who isn't here. You're a born believer, Quince. A born believer.'

'I'd be a born sucker to believe you, Noyes.'

'Suck away. And join me in my prayer, as we send the soul of Peter Comachin to intercede for us before Our Chief. Take dictation.'

Noyes picked up Comachin's obituary. And Adam became the scribe of the rites, through which the black sheep was bleached to become the sacrificial lamb on the high altar of the Chief.

BETTER DEAD IF RED?

Peter Comachin was a Commie, a killer, and a conchie. He always picked the cause that wrote out the biggest cheque. Says a highly-placed source in the Foreign Office, Comachin 'did not have the sort of reputation a diplomat can be caught dead with.'

Killer to Coward

Comachin loved a scrap, if he was well out of the front line. When things got too hot, he became a pacifist. This didn't stop him from soldiering for the Boches in the First Hun War. Only when he became a naturalized British citizen (his father's name was Rabbi Grybalowski) did Comachin squat in Trafalgar Square with a few other slackers. Once we let him in here, he wanted us to disarm against the Reds.

Close the White Cliffs

When Comachin landed here with his yellow streak, he should have been deported. We have a long and proud tradition of tolerance. But tolerance must not be confused with weakness. We have kowtowed to the Comachins of the world for too long. Close the White Cliffs of Dover now! We do not want to see his like again.

'I've kept your final sentence, Quince,' Noyes said. 'You always did have a nose for an end piece.'

With the last word said, Noyes left, triumphant as always, the obituary in his hand. Adam took a silver cigarette-case out of his pocket. He snapped the case open. The cigarettes faced each other in two white rows. Turkish on one side, Virginian on the other. Adam chose a Virginian, closed the case, and lit his cigarette from a gas-lighter. Its flame was a blue tear. It leapt up half an inch from its metal base, and hung on air, unable to fall. Adam watched it, until the gas ran out, and the blue tear became invisible.

The telephone on the desk rang. Adam lifted up the receiver, and put it in the crook of his collar-bone. One of its stubs lay against the side of his mouth, the other behind his ear.

'Morgue speaking,' Adam said.

'Noyes here again. Templeton mean anything to you?' a voice said, in the pin-cushion voice of telephones.

'Not a thing.'

'Nada Templeton.'

'The actress? Didn't I see her in . . . ?'

'You'll see her out. Car crash. She's broken her neck. In the Clinic. Get her obit ready for the next edition. We'll keep it on ice till she pips.'

'Will do.'

Adam put down the receiver from its cradle of flesh. He went over to the files, and picked out the brown envelope which carried the name, *Templeton, Nada*. The clippings inside were poor. Some theatre reviews, which said that Miss Templeton was sparkling, effervescent, bright as a champagne bubble, tinkling as a peal of bells, and promising. One interview, which stated that Nada Templeton liked children, poodles, race-horses, men who wore mohair suits, and rough cider. She did not like Alsatians, men who wore macintoshes, and cocktails. This information was copy for a story, but not for an obituary. Nada Templeton had not recorded enough to die in print.

Adam searched among the clippings for the name of a friend, who might supply an appreciation. He could find none. The actors who had appeared with her were overseas or unknown. They were also probably illiterate. They could write a few lines, perhaps, but Adam wanted more than a few lines. He could remember spending an extra sixpence in a theatre to hire an inferior pair of opera-glasses. He had wanted to look more closely at a quick girl playing the daughter in a play he had forgotten. Nada Templeton. A girl of chase and tag. A scurry in his mind.

One of the clippings carried a small photograph of Nada. She held a pose. Her face seemed flat, a cone of skin. Long dark hair covered her forehead and her cheeks. There was nothing to notice about her eyes or mouth, except that they were regular.

The telephone rang. It rang again. Adam answered.

'Morgue speaking.'

'Got anything on the girl?'

'Nothing.'

'Got anybody to do her?'

'Nobody.'

'Goddamit, Quince. Can't you even keep up with stiffs?'

'How should I know every time there's a young bit about to croak? How about you doing some leg-work for a change, Noyes? Or have you broken your crutches?'

''Nuff said, Quince. You've been so long in the Morgue we'd forgotten where we buried you.'

'Put me back on the London History column again,' Adam said. 'I'm an old friend of Julius Caesar. Or even the Sports Page.'

'Sorry. We need a live-wire there, not a cadaver. I'll see if I can get a man to the Clinic, though we're pushed Saturdays . . .'

'I'll go,' Adam said. He had not known until he spoke that he would go.

'You're sure you can stand the shock, Quince? It's light up here.'

'I'll remember to order new eyes.'

'And, Quince, one last thing. We'll be good to you. You can charge the hearse to expenses.'

2

THE summer sun did hurt Adam Quince's eyes. Although he put on his dark glasses, he still felt pain in his head. He turned into the bar of Father's off Fleet Street. Forty reporters and editors were between him and his need. He knew them all. It took him fifteen minutes to buy his double gin, and one minute to drink it.

'Crime is the curse of the drinking classes,' Nobble said, fat and red and wrapped in tweed. 'Blessed be murder, for it restoreth our circulation. But damned is he who writes of murder. His feet shall drop off and his throat shall grow dry and he shall report, Blood, blood everywhere, and never a drop to drink.'

'Why aren't you ferreting through Camden Town?' Adam said. 'On the trail of the new Ripper.'

Nobble looked past the wart on his nose, and laid his finger upon it to keep it in place. 'I have a hunch,' he said, 'that the Ripper will strike again here. On Elsie.' He pointed to the barmaid, who looked more likely to puncture than bleed.

'Perhaps he'll change his tastes and rip me,' Adam said. 'In which case, *you* . . .'

'You'd like to have me in the Morgue, wouldn't you?' Nobble said. 'Then you could have my job.'

Adam laughed.

'Crime doesn't pay, except its reporter's expenses.'

Through the crowd, Noyes pushed, lean as a strop, his glass eye bigger and brighter in the bar light than his red own.

'Lost your way, Quince? Or are they bringing the Clinic down here brick by brick?'

'Our sleuth is telling me how to get there by following the mud on people's boots.'

'Follow the coffin, Quince. Follow the coffin. That's where the story's to be found.'

'You're a damned grave-digger, Noyes,' Nobble said.

'I am not. I am not.' The glass eye spun in its socket, spick as a silver coin. 'I don't want bodies from you. I want resurrection. You are the truth and the life. Make the dead speak. By their tongues, we shall know them. And you are their tongues. Did they rack, did they rent, did they screw? You shall tell us, Nobble. Did they cant, did they anger, did they breed? You shall tell us, Quince. Crime and obit, the quick and the dead.' The finger of Noyes stabbed the air faster than a type-setter. 'Do you groan in the Morgue, my poor old Quince? You should grin. Through your files, the whole world marches. You can look them up living, and sew them down lost and gone before. Smile, Quince, smile. You're recorder, jury and judge. No one enters into the printed heaven of the dear departed without your saving grace. Now get the hell to that Clinic, and grab that soul on the wing.'

Adam drifted out of Father's into the street. The gin was sea in his head. The heat of exhaust was stale brine in his nose. He held up a hand in the gesture of a drowning man, as a black boat swam down the roadway. It pulled up.

'The Clinic,' Adam said.

Inside, the leather of the taxi seat was warm. It was the hide of a beast to Adam's hands, as he rubbed them dry. He looked out, down Kingsway. Red, pink, orange, green, white, the secretaries and shoppers flaunted their dresses. Black and grey the men answered their sobersides. But the sun had striped and flecked them all in tawny hairs. The traffic roared as a zoo.

New tar had been laid on the pavement in the street by the Clinic. A man knelt on the kerb. He was ironing the tar. As Adam turned away from paying off the cab, he saw smoke rise in the sun under the sweeps of the iron. The man's body opened as a book while he brought the iron back from railing to kerb. He ironed on and on, shifting his knees along the stone border of the pavement. If grace were economy of movement, this man had grace. If grace were more, why should not grace be in the power of the ironer of the street, where all men walked?

Adam had difficulty with the woman who sat in the chair of Reception. Her concern seemed less to receive than to reject.

'There is no Miss Templeton here,' she said firmly.

'Is it a stage name?'

'Don't you know? There is a Joyce Howell, who calls herself Nada Templeton.'

'Then may I see Miss Howell?'

'Are you a close personal friend or relative of hers?'

'Not exactly.'

'Are you from the newspapers?'

'Not exactly.'

'There is no use waiting. Her condition is unchanged. While she is in danger, only family may see her.'

'I don't write gossip. I have to do her obituary.'

The face of the woman in Reception softened. Obituary had the sound of surgery, autopsy, mortuary. Respectable words.

'Her obituary is different.'

'Unique, ma'am.'

At this title, given only to queens and dames at Eton College, the woman softened further.

'You will have to speak to the sister in charge of the corridor.'

She wrote a number and a letter on a piece of paper, and handed it to Adam.

'I promise not to disturb her,' Adam said.

'I always wondered how the details of the departed were so prompt in the papers.'

'Hard work, ma'am, and insight, and, above all, the kindness of the living.'

Adam smiled at the woman in Reception, and turned towards the lift. Its doors were closed against him. He pressed the summoning button, and scowled. Machinery did not need flattery. Adam had always kept his charm for door-keepers and secretaries. There was no other way to the great. Even St Peter had to be persuaded before a man could interview God.

The lift doors opened. A woman walked past Adam. She wore a grey silk dress, grey gloves, grey shoes, a grey bag. A white bandage round her neck, supporting her long chin on a pink plate, broke the colour of her choosing. She carried her head carefully and still. It lay on its platter of cloth, apart from her body. Only her hair, grey but streaked with white, suggested that her clothes and head belonged to each other.

Adam entered the lift. He pressed the button for the seventh floor. The doors closed without noise. The lift rose. Adam felt the unease of small, closed, moving spaces. The lift might stop between

floors. The cable of the lift might part. The lift might be broken on
the concrete base of its shaft. The lift might rise and rise, until the
cage toppled the roof and spilled him on to the parapets. Travel in
a lift for Adam did not suppose arrival.

The lift arrived. The doors opened. Adam walked out into the
corridor. He was alone. Dark walls, dark ceilings, dark doors, dark
passages stretched on either side of him towards windows, where
the white light of the sun made dark the hospital paint. Only at the
very door bearing the letter and number of the paper in his hand
could Adam see that the colour of the wood was cream.

He knocked at the door. There were steps within. For a moment,
Adam imagined Nada appearing, holding her head upright in her
hands. Absurd. The door opened a small way. A thin man of middle
height looked at Adam. He was beautiful.

Adam had never conceived of a beautiful man before. The man
had a pure pale skin. His pallor even seemed to have drained the
blue of his eyes into their lids. His nostrils were as perfect as the
folded wings of a moth. Only his lips were a little too narrow. His
age was indeterminate. On his high forehead, white hair grew as
careless and free as a young man's. There were no wrinkles in his
face except for a line of intention at the corner of his mouth.

'You wish?' the man said.

'Miss Templeton, I presume?'

'You do. The name?'

'She won't know me.'

'Then she still will not.'

The man began to close the door.

'I am from the insurance,' Adam said.

'The *life* insurance?'

'Yes.'

'Can you *insure* she will live?' the man said. The line on his mouth
irritated Adam. By the bed of the dying, irony?

'Are you a friend of hers?'

'More or less,' the man said. 'Or rather, more and less.'

A voice spoke from inside the room. It was weary, and spoke in
pain.

'Who's that?'

'Your insurance man, Nada.'

'I don't have one.'

The man smiled at Adam.

'Does she now? Or do you impost?'

'I impost,' Adam said. He put on his own smile of charm. 'May I have a word with you outside?'

The man looked at Adam, then nodded. He turned away.

'Excuse me,' he said. 'I will not be away from you for long.'

He came out of the room, and closed the door behind him. He stood very still in perfect outline against the cream paint. He seemed to have chosen a flattering frame for himself.

'Are you a journalist?'

'No,' Adam said.

'If you are an agent,' the man said, 'it is not a good time to approach your future client. She could only accept lie-in parts.'

Again Adam felt a prick of irritation.

'It's not a joking matter,' he said.

'Isn't it?'

The man laughed softly. Only his mouth moved. His body retained its posture of easy immobility. His lack of motion seemed to be a mockery of the ill and the dying and the paralysed behind the other doors of the Clinic.

Down the corridor, a nurse wheeled an old woman in a chair. The old woman turned her head from side to side, seeking.

'Nurse,' she said, 'Nurse.'

'Yes, dear,' the nurse said.

'Do you know . . . ?' The old woman forgot what she was saying. Her head turned again, looking for the question.

'Yes, dear,' the nurse said, to be kind. With her left hand, she pressed back the old woman's head against the pillow on the chair. The old woman lay still. She forgot to move. The nurse wheeled her on.

'If you could help me,' Adam said with distaste.

'Perhaps,' the man said.

'My job . . .'

'You work, do you?' the man said. 'I should have known.' The sneer in his voice was too faint to be an insult.

'Yes. Doesn't everybody?' Adam said.

'The unfortunate must.'

'And the poor,' Adam said.

'Naturally. The poor. Yet this is an odd place for a poor man to beg, isn't it?' The man's tone of tender inquiry was a refinement of mockery. 'I know the dying cannot take it with them, as the saying goes. But relatives usually expect it first. Perhaps you know Nada has no relatives?'

'I am not a beggar.' Adam found it hard to control his voice.

'I apologize,' the man said. 'Of course you are a chooser. You chose to come here. What is your trade?'

'I organize obituaries,' Adam said, with embarrassment.

The man looked at Adam. Until now, the line on the edge of his mouth had been a bar to the intruder. It now fell into his lips in delight. He even leaned a little towards Adam, and disturbed his pose.

'Really?' the man said. He laughed as easily as a child, in wonder and pleasure. 'You organize obituaries? You lay out the memory of the dead?'

'We haven't enough on Miss Templeton.' Adam was determined to explain as a professional. He would not play the part of an acquaintance. 'It's wrong that people should die without telling other people about themselves. It wouldn't be fair on her, after all her efforts. It would seem a wasted life.'

'Like mine,' the man said. Then he bowed slightly. 'But never like yours.'

'Can I see Miss Templeton then?'

'Of course. Under what mask of gladness?'

'An admirer.'

'You have actually bothered to see her act?' The tone of the man's voice had changed to one of amused courtesy. 'Of course. One must prepare for the joy to come.'

'Yes. I remember her moving. Just her moving.'

'Not now,' the man said. He stood stiffly for a moment. Then he moved his hand for the first time in minutes, in order to take a card out of the breast-pocket of his light-grey suit, with its stripes so thin that they teased the eye. 'Here is my address. Perhaps this evening . . .'

'I'm going out.' As Adam said this, he looked at the card. It read:

John Purefoy
Gentleman

It also gave an address in Belgravia.

'Late this evening,' the man said. 'After midnight?'

'It would be keeping you up.'

'I never sleep early, because I toil not, neither do I spin.'

'I do,' Adam said, 'as you know. So perhaps . . .'

'You would like the details of Nada's life.' The man did not ask Adam. He knew the answer. Irony again stropped his tone.

'Yes. Are you sure that tonight . . .'

'Certain,' the man said. He grasped the handle of the door of the room. The skin of his hand was whiter than the cream of the paint. His nails seemed to glint. 'I must go back to my duty.'

'And I to mine,' Adam said.

'At twelve,' the man said. 'And your name?'

'Adam Quince.'

'Adam?'

The man opened the door of the room wide as he entered. He seemed to move deliberately behind the door, as though to clear the stage for Adam's view. Under a sheet on an iron bed, a body lay, sloping upwards slightly from the line of the mattress. The profile of a girl's face, set exactly parallel to the line of her body, lay on a raised pillow. A metal harness supported her neck. A steel wire ran up from her crown of dark hair over a pulley on the rail of the bed-head. From the pulley, the wire ran down to a lead weight as large as a melon.

Nada Templeton could not move. Only the door moved, which shut her necessary stillness from Adam.

3

THE room was known and unfamiliar as the rooms of rich aunts are known and unfamiliar. The aunts may be visited often, but their setting remains alien and uncomforting. Each time that Adam came into Lottie's sitting-room, he felt wary of the corruption behind such luxury.

The chairs hardly seemed able to carry their own weight. Their legs were starved. Their Chippendale style was in such perfect condition that it whispered forgery. The sofa, with its thin scrolls and yellow brocade cover, bore pleats of reproach every time a guest disturbed the soft flank of its seat. The varnish on the paintings on the wall brought out the deceit of the *trompe l'œil* flower-pieces, but destroyed their intention. They seemed too careful to be more than artificial. The pile of the sand-coloured carpet left no print of a shoe. Even the long folds of the green silk curtains were regular, giving them the quality of pillars. They were not meant to cover the windows, but to frame them. Only the daylight, reflected off the glass prisms of the chandelier, worried the complacent eye. Yet a close look revealed that the source of annoyance was an exquisite and inverted pyramid.

When there were visitors, Lottie's entrance into her sitting-room was precise. She knew her place in her surroundings as she knew her status in the universe. She was rightly where she chose to be. The visitor was shown in by the maid, who had instructions to leave him facing the windows. Adam duly stood on his proper spot.

Through the door from her bedroom, Lottie swam and turned, keeping the daylight behind her. She wore green muslin, which seemed to sheathe the body of a young girl. But there were so many scarves sewn on her dress that their coils round throat and shoulder and waist hid the thick lines of breast and belly.

The light from the windows put a match to the careful red of Lottie's hair. And Adam, blinded by the brightness, could only see the features that Lottie wanted to be seen. The orange definition of her lips. The eyes slicked by drops into brilliance. And the strange black arcs of her eyebrows, two silhouettes of domes painted higher than the shaven skin of her proper brow.

Lottie gave her usual start of surprise. She refused to count on the expected or the inevitable. Even old age might not call upon her.

'Darling,' she said, 'it's you. My dear, dear boy.'

She put her hand lightly on Adam's forearm. At first she seemed only to want a dark cloth pad for the display of the five silver trowels of her nails. But then she tightened her fingers. Adam could feel their tips exploring the sinews under his skin. Lottie could never have enough of young thew.

'Surely you were not expecting somebody else?' Adam said.

'Oh, you never know . . .'

Lottie turned, and ran a step or two away from Adam, as though in love with moving, as if her limbs had to work, as at sixteen. But when she reached the sofa and sat on its forward edge, her back straight against a shelf of air, she pressed her knees together and smoothed her dress over them as carefully as a dowager.

Adam again felt the irritation which he had sensed at the hospital. These bloody rich. All the manners money could buy. Well preserved, well bred, well dead.

'You knew it was me coming,' he said. 'You were just playing up.'

'It could have been anyone,' Lottie said. 'But I'm thrilled it was you. Come and sit beside me. Here.'

She patted the white seat as if to encourage a Pekinese to jump up.

'I'll stand, thanks. I want to stretch my legs.'

Adam was lying. He was tired, and his legs were weak.

'Don't be a mean thing.'

Lottie made her pretty face. It appealed. But the cracks round the nose and mouth and eye underlined the appeal.

'I'm not mean, Lottie. I just happen to want to do something you don't.'

'Don't let's quarrel. I haven't seen you since yesterday.'

'If you were made to get up earlier . . .'

'I need my beauty sleep.'

At the word 'beauty' applied to herself, Lottie threw up her chin so that a little of the daylight lay along the good line of her jawbone.

'All the sleep in the world wouldn't make much difference now,' Adam said. He squared his shoulders back, conscious of dominance.

'Mean again. Very mean.'

'I'm not mean. Just truthful.'

'That's always the excuse of the mean. In your little suburb . . . Where was it? . . . I forget . . .'

'Didsbury. Manchester.'

'Didsbury, didn't your mother show you her piggy-bank, stuffed with money stolen from the housekeeping, and say, Waste Not, Want Not. Only you apply it to love.'

Adam could remember his mother clearly, in front of the blue plates on the dresser of her kitchen. Indeed, there was a pink china pig with a slit in its spine for holiday money. When he generously peeled potatoes for her, she would peel the peelings. Waste Not, Want Not. It had been the first commandment of the household.

'Life's not like that in the suburbs,' Adam said in a hard voice. 'But you wouldn't know.'

'I have been to Manchester. When Ralph was alive. I launched a barge there.' Lottie laughed. 'I thought you liked to be reminded of the *good earth* where you are from.'

'My father was a farmer.'

'A farm labourer, surely.'

'He had a plot of his own. If he had to move into the city . . .'

'Lucky he did, wasn't it? Ambitious youths always tread on Manchester in their scramble to get to London.'

'I'm proud of where I come from.'

'Is that why your accent tries so hard to forget it?'

'You bitch, Lottie.'

Lottie's tone changed. She patted the seat again.

'Now be a good boy. Sit. Sit.'

'I'm not a dog.'

'Sit. Sit.'

Adam came across to the sofa. He did not know why he came. The young should have the power over the ageing. Surely thirty years could put the screws on forty-nine. The old were the disinherited of the earth. And yet he obeyed. This was proof that he was kind, after all.

As Adam sat down, he gave Lottie a sharp slap across her thigh, to disarrange her pose. She yelped and was angry.

'Why do that?'

'To squash a fly.'

'If there had really been one, it would have ruined my dress.'

'Then you would have had to take it off.'

At his suggestion, Adam could see Lottie's anger melting into amorousness. The slap had been a stimulation.

'Mean, but . . . if you meant . . .'

Adam smiled, secure in his power again.

'Meant for a fly, my love.'

He bent and kissed the side of Lottie's neck. To his lips, her skin was girlish. But he kept his eyes open to note the web of wrinkles on her cheek.

'You naughty child,' Lottie said to his hair.

'I need my girl.'

'Your woman, you mean.'

'My baby.'

Adam could feel the points of Lottie's fingers pulling at the cloth of his jacket, pressing the pads of skin on his back. He knew the salt smell of victory before lust. He rose to his feet, picking up Lottie in his arms. For all the leanness of her face, she weighed heavy. His eyes calculated the twenty yards to her bedroom, and he put her on her feet again.

'Come,' he said.

'Now? You're mad. Before dinner?'

'I'll eat you.'

'No.'

But her body was already swaying towards the door of the bedroom. Adam moved in front of her, and took her with him, his arm round the rubber sheath of her waist, her red bush of hair gorse against his neck.

He took her quickly and brutally, as she liked it. He hardly undressed her. She preferred not to show her body. But his haste was not to please her. He wanted to see the coarseness of need in her face. He wanted to hear her moan after him. He wanted to study for minutes her later weariness, as she sprawled on the bed, her limbs unpinned, her lines deep, looking her age.

4

HUNGER drove Lottie and Adam from bed, the sear of hunger that
is the leaving of sex. Adam always felt grateful for Lottie's riches,
when he ate at her table. The maid had prepared an enormous
cold meal of lobster and chicken and salad and strawberries, the
conventional meal in hot weather for Lottie's circle. There was
also champagne to drink. Adam still marvelled that champagne
could be treated as an ordinary wine, to be enjoyed. He was used
to the slight explosion of the cork as the first shot in the duty of
celebration. But champagne tasted better as something to wash
down daily bread.

Lottie proved difficult to leave after dinner. She would not believe that Adam could be seeing a man at midnight. She examined
the visiting-card which Adam produced, and laughed.

'John Purefoy, Gentleman. No gentleman would dream of putting Gentleman after his name.'

'He acts like he thought he was one.'

'And Purefoy, what a false surname! Pure foi, unspotted faith! In
what? His own pretences?'

'He's a phoney, for sure.'

'Then why see him?'

'I need him for an obituary.'

'Work? At midnight?'

'He can't see me at any other time.'

'And if I said I couldn't see you at any other time?'

'You can, my love. At all times.'

'Don't be too sure.'

Lottie's words were no threat. They were merely a concession
to her pride.

*   *   *

Purefoy lived ten minutes away from Lottie's door. Adam's walk
lay through the pillared squares of Georgian London. Everywhere,

the white steps and white walls and large windows of Belgravia outlined their definition of riches. Wealth had a sharp edge, a clean shirt, an open stare, a closed door. Wealth lived in a spacious box, looking inwards upon itself. Wealth enclosed a private park with high wire and gates, for which it alone had the key. Wealth suffered the many to use the street; this was their right of way because their duty was to serve wealth. Adam could only lose his envy of wealth in the admiration of what it could own.

Purefoy's house was, naturally, different from those of its neighbours. It was a cottage among houses, two storeys stooping beneath five, brick among stone, a survival and a polite snook at the great. The fact that it had outlived the vast rebuilding of Belgravia proved its superiority by its lowliness. The holiest of saints are beggars. A man who could afford to live alone in this valuable patch had proved his worth. He had paid as much for his cottage as he would have for two mansions. And he could claim all the good taste that lack of ostentation can buy.

There was no bell to the house, only a black iron knocker on the door. The knocker was in the shape of a cross. It bore the legend, AND YE SHALL AWAKEN THE DEAD.

'Damn him,' Adam said aloud. He swung the iron knocker repeatedly and loudly.

'Who is it?' a voice said by Adam's ear. Adam started. Then he saw that a grid had been placed in the mouth of a grotesque devil's face to the right of the door. He spoke into the grid.

'Adam Quince.'

There was a burr of sound at the door. It opened. No bell, Adam thought, and an electrically-operated door. The precious bastard.

Adam walked into the lighted hall. It was the house of a collector of knick-knacks. The walls were hung with trophies. Two dolls, cut out of white paper, skeletons inside the clothes of bride and groom, led the Mexican dance of death. Georgian embroidered pictures of girls beside weeping willows spelt out a forgotten grief on the stitches of funeral urns.

Adam paused to read the inscription on one of the embroidered tombs:

In
Affectionate Remembrance
Of EMMA FISHER
Who Departed This Life
Oct. The I.st 1807
Aged 4 Years
Not Lost But Gone
Before

A chiming clock began to strike in a room. Its noise was faint, but became louder on the third stroke as a door opened into the hall. John Purefoy appeared. He was wearing a black silk jacket and dark trousers and black suede slippers. Round his neck, a black scarf was tucked into a charcoal shirt. In his buttonhole, one white camellia. He paused for effect, until the seventh stroke.

'How prompt, Mr Quince. Midnight precisely. Do please come in. Abandon hope all ye that enter here. I would have a plaque engraved over the door, if it were not so trite. Or so exact.'

He led the way into the sitting-room, which was again a trove of curios rather than a hive or a home. Adam deliberately refused to let his attention wander off Purefoy. He would not give his host the pleasure of looking at his belongings.

'What will you drink, Mr Quince?'

'Whisky would do. Straight. On the rocks.'

'Pray excuse me, while I prepare it.'

Purefoy left the room. Adam stayed alone for five minutes. For the first two, his determination kept his attention on his own thumbs, which he twiddled with concentration. But the cleverness of Purefoy had allowed no newspaper, no magazine, no wireless, no television, nothing to remain in the room that might distract the visitor's eye from bookcase or shelf or wall. Boredom forced Adam first to light a cigarette, and then to look at the chimney-piece.

Over the fire-place, there hung a painting showing the naked infant Jesus asleep on a gravestone in the shape of a cross. On the cross was carved QUO VADIS?

On the chimney-piece itself, five objects were spaced carefully.

The first was the small miniature of a wooden skull set in a box ornamented with flowers. A painted inscription read, ÉGALITÉ.

The next was another skull, larger and carved in ivory, with a snake coiling in and out of the sockets of mouth and nose and eye and ear.

The third was a complex piece of Staffordshire china. Two gentlemen in green coats, carrying a sword and a book between them, stood facing a black message – PREPARE TO MEET THY GOD. Above them, the sun and moon showed their rosy faces on either side of a clock, outlined in flames, perpetually stopped at thirteen minutes to twelve. On the curved top of the piece, four angels' faces flew between wings, and a cherub leaned on a tomb of stone, bearing the legend, TIME FLYES.

The fourth object was the skeleton of a bat, its picked bones delicate as the fibres of a white leaf, encased in an oblong of glass.

The last thing on the chimney-piece was incongruous. It seemed to be a china, wigged Pompadour in a hoop skirt. Adam approached it with relief, admiring the easy shine of the yellow and green and pink glazes, on hat and bodice and flesh. It was the ornament which Adam expected on the shelves of the rich – the pleasant and dear. But as he looked down the ridges of the hooped skirt, he saw that the china had been cut away as at the opening of a tent. The frame of the hoops was exposed. Peering out of its cage, a jade Fabergé toad sat, winking one ruby eye.

'How do you like my trivialities?' Purefoy said behind Adam.

'Very commonplace, aren't they?' Adam said curtly. He took his glass of whisky, and drank a long swallow.

'Unfortunately, it takes a lifetime to acquire the commonplace,' Purefoy said. Then he added, with a sweet smile, 'For those not born to it.'

'What are we born to?' Adam said, rhetorically.

'To die.' Purefoy smiled again.

'I mean, born to *be*. Nothing. You're what you make of yourself.'

'And what do you make of yourself, Mr Quince?'

Adam was damned if he would be drawn into a game of confidences.

'Just what you see.'

'I wish I could say the same,' Purefoy said sadly. 'Unfortunately,

I can make nothing of myself. I know that I am merely what I was born. I really have no option. Nor, I fear, have you.'

'Nonsense. I can do what I please.'

'Within narrow limits. Our species is rather confined. We must eat, sleep, lust – although I agree this goes at my age – and some say, we must work. And, of course, suffer.'

'Suffer? What for?'

'There have been perpetual insomniacs, fasters for more than forty days, monks sworn to chastity and even chaste, and total idlers like myself. But one thing we all have in common. Suffering. That is why I collect what you rightly called the commonplace, things to remind me that we must suffer.'

Adam laughed.

'You're what we call precious, Mr Purefoy, aren't you? A lot of palaver over nothing. Of course, we've all got to go and we bang a hammer on our thumbs from time to time. But just because you don't enjoy yourself, you can't lump in the rest of humanity with your own failings.'

'You really are fascinating, Mr Quince. You write obituaries, and you stay cheerful. That means, either you share the most enviable quality of the human race, its ability to dance even while it is being hanged. Or else you are one of the few like myself, who pass their apathy – miscalled life – finding a little amusement in the folly of their fellows.'

'I'm just not morbid,' Adam said. 'If you did a proper job, you wouldn't have time to think up all this crap. Look, could we talk about Nada? That's my job, and what I came for.'

A hint of surprise or distaste crossed Purefoy's smooth cheek.

'Oh yes. Nada. I had forgotten her. Which, I will admit, was a little premature, since she is not yet dead.'

Purefoy went across to a black leather sofa, sat down, hitched up his trousers so as not to spoil their crease, and crossed his legs fastidiously. He then extended his fingers, placed their tips together, and balanced his chin on his thumbs. The effect was of four bars of flesh below his mouth. It was as if he had dropped a vizor of skin to reveal his true face.

'I shall keep no secrets in front of the recorder of the dead.'

'Dying.'

'Dying, Mr Quince. Correct as always. Though in time, dead.'

'Is she better?'

'The hospital says, still critical.'

'Then could you tell me something about her?'

'I should warn you, Mr Quince, that I know nothing about anybody. Therefore, I cannot write an obituary for you, only describe a few events. As I presume to mock the antics of the human race, I dare not seek their motives. Who knows?' His face showed mock horror. 'I might *pity* them.'

'When did you meet Nada?' Adam asked.

'Several years ago. I found myself in Henley one evening. I can't imagine why – I must have lost my way. I wandered into an attempt at a theatre there. I say, an attempt, because although the curtain rose and the actors mouthed lines, there was no performance as recognized in the Western world, and no audience except myself. Nada, or rather Joyce as she was then . . .'

'Why did she change her name?'

'At my suggestion, Mr Quince. Nada means Nothing. Templeton, a place of worship in a town. Appropriate, I thought, for someone who wanted to worship in front of that empty altar, the stage. And live inside her own skull, as she must.'

'I'm surprised she agreed with you.'

'When I found her, she was practically illiterate.'

'Do you like playing Pygmalion?' Adam said, pleased at his own literary knowledge.

'It amuses me.'

Adam had smoked his cigarette down to the butt. He balanced it upright between finger and thumb, preserving a pillar of grey ash on the surface of the smouldering tobacco. He looked round for an ash-tray; but the order of the room did not provide any receptacle for the normal litter of living.

Purefoy saw Adam's plight. He dropped his hands from his chin, and rose, uncrossing his legs with the delicacy of a woman rising to acknowledge a curtsy. He walked over to a shelf and put out his hand to grasp the china hand of an ash-tray, which held up its palm for the remainders of cigarettes. He came across to Adam and placed the china hand on the exact centre of the glass top of the round table in front of his guest. The ash-tray now covered the card of the Hanged Man from the old fortune-telling tarot pack, set out below the glass on the table as the hub of a wheel of tarot cards. Purefoy then returned to his seat, and sat down with exactly the same series of movements that he used before, ending with the balancing of his chin on his thumbs.

Adam saw that Purefoy, in every minor action, calculated its effect. Each gesture of his was as deliberate as each piece of furniture or china. He never seemed to scratch his nose or pull the lobe of his ear or bite his nails or push his hair back into place. He performed none of the careless actions that proclaim a human personality. His only mannerism seemed to be to exclude mannerisms. He remained perpetually still, upright, attentive. He never changed his mind. Once his hands moved, they moved only to fulfil a chosen purpose. Every function was carried out with all due speed, without fumbling. Purefoy lived precisely within the yard of his intentions, or pretensions. He was flawless in his showmanship of himself. The marionette that he wished to be, sat, moved, did, spoke, for its master within itself.

'And Nada?' Adam said. 'What did she think of you? Was she really your puppet, or were you hers?'

Purefoy smiled his thin smile.

'Like you, Mr Quince, I prefer not to discuss more than is necessary. You wished to know about Nada. I will give you some details.' For the first time, Purefoy's voice became brisk and matter of fact. 'She comes from Barnsley originally. Then from a series of army camps. She is an orphan. Her real name is Joyce Howell. There is no point in dwelling on the misery of her early life. All children are miserable.'

'I had a happy childhood.'

'In retrospect. Have you ever seen those bare-kneed herds of infants at the bus-stop, winter in and winter out, at crack of dawn, waiting to go to a school they hate? If you have, you have a definition of human misery. Well, Nada escaped to Henley. And escaped from Henley to London.'

'You helped her?'

'Not really. I encouraged her to come to London. For a time, she left the stage, if you can say that she had ever been upon it.'

'What did she live on?'

Purefoy dropped his hands to his lap, and shrugged.

'Really. What a question!'

'It's the only one, isn't it?' Adam said.

'It has never occurred to me.'

'Has poverty ever occurred to you?'

Again distaste made a furrow on Purefoy's cheek.

'No. But, really, I do apologize, a gentleman cannot refer to these matters . . .'

'A gentleman?' Adam said. 'Oh yes, your card *said* so.'

'It is the simple truth. Others may put Poet after their name, or Plumber, or the Collection of Capital Letters that people acquire when they give up hope and join the closed profession of their successful inferiors. I put Gentleman. I am, you know, Mr Quince, a real one. Sometimes, I think, the *last* gentleman.'

'I don't know about that,' Adam said, 'but then I don't know about gentlemen.'

'They are not common now,' Purefoy said. 'But we were speaking of Miss Templeton.'

'I said, what did she live on after she came here?'

'I cannot answer that question.'

'Because once you know what somebody lives on,' Adam said, 'you know all.'

'You live on the death of others, Mr Quince. Do I know all?'

'It's a job like any other,' Adam said.

'To live on death?'

'You live on dead meat. Does it worry you? No. And my job doesn't worry me. I need the money. What did Nada do for money?'

Purefoy brought up the palm of one hand and yawned deliberately.

'I have kept you too long already, Mr Quince. Thank you for gracing my home.'

'Oh no,' Adam said, 'you dragged me here at midnight. I thought I was your recorder of death. Entitled to the truth.'

'The truth, like my patience, has its limits. We have reached them. I would not dream of telling you about Miss Templeton's private affairs.'

'You kept her,' Adam said. 'She was your mistress.'

With his right hand, Purefoy took off, finger by finger, an invisible glove from his left hand. He then rose, walked over to Adam, and struck at his face. Adam brought up his own hands against the blow. But Purefoy's palm passed an inch or two in front of his nose.

'I do not wear gloves indoors, Mr Quince. Thus I fear my slap was symbolic. But intentional.'

'What's my symbolic answer?' Adam said. 'Do I challenge you to a duel with penknives at forty paces?'

Purefoy smiled. He spoke more slowly than usual, stressing his words to emphasize either their irony or their seriousness.

'One of us will have to die now, Mr Quince. And not symbolically. I agree, all honour may be a myth. But it demands a real sacrifice.'

'I suppose I'll be punctured to death by the rapiers of your wit,' Adam said.

'Words are the best murderers,' Purefoy said, 'when they are considered, and believed.'

There was a pause. Adam wanted to destroy Purefoy's pretensions. Purefoy must be her lover. He had been admitted to Nada's hospital room. For all his taste for the bizarre, he was predictable. Or the habits of his money and his class and his code were.

'You kept Nada, didn't you?' Adam said. 'And she got fed up with being a rich man's mistress. She wanted a job of her own. So she left you, got a break, went back on the stage, began to make it. And broke her neck.'

Purefoy smothered another yawn.

'If your obituaries match your speculations, you will outdo Our Lord. All the dead will have to rise again to deny your perjuries.'

'It's true,' Adam said. 'That's what finishes you *gentlemen*. We want jobs. We like doing them. We're damned if we'll be kept on what's been pinched from the past.'

Purefoy clapped his hands together once. They made a soft noise, like the closing of a book.

'Isn't your name Adam?'

'It's not significant. *I* didn't choose it.'

'The first man. He who committed the original sin. Or should I say, the first of the new men?'

'No. My name doesn't mean a thing. I'm just one of the crowd. Except I'm getting out of the crowd. They'll choke in my dust.'

Purefoy dropped his hand lightly on Adam's shoulder, as if posing for a photograph.

'The first man,' he said, 'and the last gentleman? A conceit. A pretty conceit.'

Adam finished his whisky.

'I'll be off,' he said. 'I've got to get to work in the morning.'

'May I visit you one day?' Purefoy asked. 'I would be fascinated.'

'If you like,' Adam said. 'On one condition.'

'Anything, my dear fellow.'

'If you will introduce me to Nada, when she gets better.'

Purefoy paused, and then mocked him.

'Isn't your hope rather stronger than her nature?'

'Perhaps. But people do recover from broken necks these days. Medicine's getting so far ahead it'll end by making us live for ever.'

'Don't depress me,' Purefoy sighed. 'I agree to your condition.'

'There's one string. I don't want Nada to know what I do. I wouldn't like her to think I just wanted to meet her to do my job.'

'Why not? I thought you were proud of your work.'

'There's such a thing as tact,' Adam said. 'Tell what I do, to an ill girl?'

Purefoy laughed out loud.

'I fear the gentleman is sneaking up in you, Mr Quince. Your delicacy amuses me. I will not tell Nada what your job is.' Purefoy paused. 'On my word of honour as a gentleman.'

5

ADAM sat at his desk, slitting open letters with his thumb.

Dear Sir,
    I feel I cannot take over the duty of keeping up the obituary of my dear friend, George Clark. His death is too painful a subject to be considered . . .

Adam put the letter in a wire cage marked CHICKENS, and slit open another letter.

Dear Sir,
    I still have not received the annual payment of five guineas for keeping up the obituary of Sir Evelyn Gracewell . . .

Adam threw the letter into another wire cage, marked CROWS. Between the cowardly and the greedy, the world was divided. There was a third wire basket in front of Adam; but this was rarely used. It was marked MILCH COWS. It was for those who wrote:

Dear Sir,
    I accept the painful task of keeping up the obituary of my dear friend. His worth should be recognized at his death. I must refuse, however, any payment. There can be no question of money in this sad duty . . .

The telephone on Adam's desk rang.
    'Morgue speaking.'
    'Good piece of yours,' Noyes said. 'I liked that bit about, From Nothing to Something. Any Schoolgirl Can Be Her Own Star. That's what Mary Q. Public wants to think of heaven. It might make Page Three, if she gets better.'
    'Unsigned?'
    'You'll get a by-line next year.'

'Sure. From Our Special Co-Respondent.'

'I thought rich *widows* were your speciality,' Noyes said. 'You get galloping insomnia unless you sleep with someone else's bank roll.'

'I'd rather be rich myself. I'm putting in for ten quid expenses.'

'We'll allow you five. Or you'll get ideas above your station.'

'I'd settle for doing Horoscopes, to get out of this cellar.'

'When's your birthday?' Noyes said.

'Do I get a raise? January 21st.'

'Aquarius. The water-carrier. I read your future, Quince. It's deep in drizzle. I see a dark girl, and a long journey, and the death of someone near and dear to you. Cross my palm with thirty pieces of silver, and I'll see more. I'll see your crucifixion.'

The telephone went dead. Noyes always wanted the last word, and he was successful.

Adam had hardly put down the receiver, when the telephone rang again.

'Morgue speaking.'

There was a laugh in the receiver.

'Delightful, Mr Quince. Morgue speaking, it is too good to be true. I have sad news for you.'

'Purefoy?'

'The same.'

'Nada, she's dead?'

'Worse than that. She is better.'

'I told you.'

'We may hope for a relapse. Otherwise, I fear she is out of danger.'

'Can I see her?'

'What is she to you, Mr Quince? You have never explained.'

'I told you. I liked to see her moving. You said you'd introduce me.'

'I shall be there between four and five. Visiting hours. I shall explain that you are a friend of mine and an admirer of hers. No more.'

'I'll bring flowers,' Adam said.

'A wreath? How very thoughtful.'

The telephone again went dead before Adam could reply. But

he did not feel cheated. There was the strange flutter in his blood
that meant a flight into chaos. He would buy her roses. Red roses.
Joyce Howell would appreciate those.

*   *   *

Greyness was molten over London. Grey had spilled from the
sky over the stone, over the windows, plating them with metal,
over the armoured skins of the passers-by. The pavements were
sheets of iron, reflecting the sky. The noise of drills digging up the
roadway made the street into a foundry. As he walked the last half-
mile towards the Clinic and the summer dust scuffed his trousers,
Adam wished he were wearing overalls. The buds of the roses in
his hand were luckily protected by a plastic hood; but even they
were so weary that they had forgotten to open.

The woman at Reception let Adam through without protest.
She was charmed by his thoroughness. 'I hope you take as much
care with me,' she said, 'when it's my time to go.'

Adam knocked lightly on the cream door of Joyce's room. It
opened at once. Purefoy might have been waiting behind the door
for the knock.

'Mr Quince. I have told Nada of your coming. Please enter.'

Adam came into the room. He looked over to the bed. Joyce
still lay without moving. The weight on its wire and pulley kept
her head flat against the frame under her back. Adam saw a plaster cast round her neck above the sheet. The cast was a cup to
her face. Above, a mouth smiled to see the roses. And two amber
eyes moved after Adam's movements, curious and sufficient as two
goldfish in two ponds.

'My name is Adam Quince. I have often seen you act. You were
so alive. Vital. I had to see you now. I hope you don't mind.'

'I'm glad,' the mouth said.

The silence of the sickroom fell upon Adam. He could not think
of a word to say. So he grinned, the lasting grin that is worn to
cheer the ill, the grin that saddens by its duration.

'Adam,' Purefoy said, 'is a new friend of mine. Our grief brings
us together. But he has been my friend, I feel, all my life.'

'Why didn't you tell me of him before?' the mouth said. 'You
love your secrets.'

'Alas, I do,' Purefoy said. 'I have to be mysterious. Because I am ashamed of having so little to hide.'

There was no concern in Purefoy's voice. His words held the studied irony of his every-day speech. Adam could not understand his brutality, and could not forgive his presence. In the loam of tenderness that the unmoving face on the bed had discovered in his heart, Adam began to hate Purefoy. The man's normality, or rather abnormality, was cruelty here. It was not only suffering that amused him. He also liked to increase pain.

'I agree with you,' Adam said to Purefoy. 'I can read you like a book. A book on torture throughout the ages.'

Purefoy laughed.

'Marvellous. Will you excuse me a moment, Nada? I must find a vase and water for the roses. So original, Mr Quince. Roses. I could never have thought of it.'

He left the room on silent feet. He closed the door so gently that his going was only signalled by a slight click.

'You shouldn't have said that to the Raker,' the mouth said. 'He's very kind.'

'The Raker?'

'Yes. Didn't you know John was called the Raker? Since he was at university.'

'Why the Raker? Because he likes clawing people with his prongs?'

'Not at all. He used to have a wooden board in his rooms. He wrote on it with a poker. Some quotation from Daniel Defoe. He'll tell you. All about the plague. I don't remember it.'

'Don't talk,' Adam said, 'if it hurts you. I'd hate for you to do that.'

'Talking doesn't hurt me,' the mouth said. 'Listening does, sometimes.'

'I'm sorry, if I've said anything . . .'

'No, please. But you mustn't think badly of the Raker. I've never met anyone in my whole life so gentle. Or so kind.'

Adam looked at the still face. The eyes looked back at him, calm, with trust. Only the mouth moved, and suggested life. 'Believe me.'

'Why is it,' Adam said, 'that he's shown me nothing of this?'

'But you are his friend.'

'Yes. Even so, I thought he was a hard man.'

The mouth smiled.

'Perhaps we see ourselves in what we think are other people.'

Adam could not reply. At last he said, 'Perhaps.'

'I know,' the mouth said. 'You listen to what the Raker says. You look at his things. But those aren't him. You couldn't possibly know how much he helps me. Denying it all the time.'

'He's so damn morbid.'

'Yes. I . . . don't like . . . I know him too well to talk about him.' The mouth hesitated, closed, became dumb.

'He told me you were called Joyce,' Adam said. 'You come from the North.'

'Yes. Do you know it?'

'I come from Manchester.'

'I'm Yorkshire. Was that why you brought the red roses?'

'Yes. I wanted the roses to be from me. And they were for you.'

'I've always thought of the Wars of the Roses, Mr Quince . . .'

'Adam.'

'Adam, as a tea-party in a flower garden. People throwing roses at each other. A volley of roses. A bombardment of roses. A blitz of roses. All without thorns. Nothing but red and white and yellow flowers. And people laughing as they fight.'

'It wasn't like that.'

'No. It never is.'

Silence lay between them again. It lengthened. Purefoy came back into the room, holding a white china vase in his hand.

'I asked for alabaster,' Purefoy said, 'and they brought forth *this*. It would shame a leper's tomb.'

He put down the vase on the table by Joyce's bed. He stripped the plastic skin off the flowers. Their red buds lay in neat rows. He placed their stems in the vase, sprayed out the buds, and began arranging them in symmetry. He seemed dedicated to his task.

'I must go,' Adam said. 'I have tired you enough already.'

'It was good of you to come,' the mouth said.

'May I come again soon?'

'If you wish. I like to have somebody to talk to. And there is so much to discover in new people.'

'If you're sure that talking doesn't do you harm.'

'It's lovely to be able to move something in me,' the mouth said, 'even my lips. Goodbye.'

'Goodbye,' Adam said.

Purefoy said nothing. He concentrated on the flowers, until each stood up on its green stalk, separate, with the buds in a spread arc of red. As Adam turned back for a last look from the door, the edge of Joyce's face against the grey light on the window-pane hid the vase. The roses seemed to be sunk into her forehead and nose and mouth and chin, the shafts of arrows, their feathers bloody.

6

THE tennis ball flew above Adam. It was a meteor, a star, a sphere, a planet, a sun. He leapt. His eye was true. His hand clutched the ball in the sky, pulled it down from heaven. As his feet jarred against the earth, he fell to his knees with the shock. He now held the ball cupped in his palms.

'Saved.'

Peter ran up to his father. And Adam knew that he loved his child. This was more than the feeling that he ought to love his child, which his parents had taught him. When he saw the boy, with his cropped yellow hair, the gap in his teeth, the legs thin as railings, and his open adoration of his father, Adam's heart went out to his eight years.

The boy had been called Peter because Adam had hoped that he would become the rock-like, cocky kid, whom his father remembered or imagined himself to have been in his own youth. The very weakness of Peter had at first seemed deliberate cowardice. Now it was endearing. Adam could see the child's need of him.

'I thought that would be a goal,' Peter said.

'I should have played for Arsenal.'

'Why didn't you?'

'They wanted me, but I told them that I didn't go for their colours. I wouldn't be seen dead in red and white.' Although Adam told the story as a joke, he half hoped the boy might think it true. 'Get your coat, and we'll go and have tea with Mother.'

'Will you stay with us?'

'I'd like to,' Adam said. 'But men must work, so that little boys can play.'

Peter ran across to get one post of the goal and put it on his back. Adam went over to the other coat. The sun had made the lining warm. As he put on his jacket, the stored heat of the day glowed on his bare forearms. He might have been clothed in the hide of a fresh-killed beast.

Adam held out his hand to Peter, who hung upon it, dragging

his feet for a moment. Adam pulled him upright. They set off across the grass of the park, worn in patches to the gum. They were making for one of the villas, which surrounded the park as regularly as stopped teeth.

Every time that Adam opened the wooden gate into the front garden of Number 34, he became his son's age. He felt the murderer's guilt of a small boy, late for lunch. Then, every anticipated punishment had seemed worse than death. As a child, he had dreamed of suicide, to bring his parents weeping about his coffin, sorry at last for maltreating him. As a man, he still thought of suicide as a final justification in face of his wife, Alice. But he said to himself that her existence hung on his own. She would kill herself if she thought she bore the reproach of his death.

It was strange for Adam not to have a key to the front door. His hand automatically reached into his pocket, before it went out to press the door-bell. The broken trellis against the porch still mocked at him. He had meant to repair it daily for years. Now the opportunity was past.

Alice opened the door. Fat had made her face almost unfamiliar. It was not the fat of laughter that had puffed her cheeks and had swelled her body under her apron. It was the fat of melancholy. Even Alice's best feature, her eyes, round and mint as moons, had begun to wane under the eclipse of her lids.

'Come in. Tea's on the table.'

The kitchen reminded Adam that there was a conspiracy of kitchens. Alice had never met his mother. But she too had a dresser with its rows of blue plates; an antique table, suffering from rickets, with lace mats to preserve the scratches in its polish; and an egg-timer on the mantelpiece, spilling its slow sand. Even the introduction of a refrigerator had not led to the expulsion of an old-fashioned meat safe. All kitchens were time-machines, expresses to the past. By instinct, every woman used her kitchen to remind her husband that he was still an obedient boy.

There was little conversation at tea. Mother, father and child ate and looked at each other. Alice put food into her mouth as steadily as meat forced into a mincer. Her eyes did not seem to follow her movements. Her eating was as mechanical to her as housework. Three times she repeated, 'I really must start slimming,' and closed the sentence with a bite of fruit cake.

Peter was embarrassed by the silence. When he was allowed to leave the table and play in the garden, he ran out. He screamed like an aeroplane with the gift of wings.

'It's good of you to come and see him every week,' Alice said. 'He enjoys it.'

She began carrying the plates over to the draining-board one by one. She did not stack plates on top of each other. She thought that it doubled her work to dirty their undersides. Adam picked up a dish-towel, and waited.

'There's no reason he should suffer,' Adam said. He waited for Alice to add 'Or I', but she said nothing.

Alice ran the hot water into the double sink. She added soap powder to one of the sinks, dipped the plates in turn below the suds, scrubbed them with a plastic brush, rinsed them in clear water, and put them on the draining-board. Her movements were deft, necessary, graceful. When Adam picked up each wet hot plate, again round as a planet or sun or wheel of life, he felt the dead weight of repetition in his heart, the sinker on the days.

'I'll always be ready to take Peter out,' Adam said. 'You know I really love the child.'

'He misses you.'

'I wish I could come more often.'

'Your work must keep you busy.'

'Yes.'

'Have you got off those horrible obituaries yet?'

'Any month now.'

'Like our divorce going through.'

'Yes.'

Adam noticed that Alice could no longer use his Christian name, as he could not use hers. Familiarity was already more feared between them than separation. And yet he was familiar with this alien woman and her alien house. He knew the right drawer for every knife and fork.

'How much longer can you stay?'

'The train goes in half an hour.'

'There's a train every half an hour.'

'I should catch the next one.'

'If you ought to.'

Alice fell into her melancholy again. And Adam returned to his guilt. Every time he came into the house, guilt was a wasp about his head. At each frequent silence of Alice, the wasp crawled over his puckering skin. He could grow angry at his guilt; but he dare not crush it, for fear of its sting.

Alice's melancholy was his doing. Or perhaps she was sick in her mind. A natural depressive. Not certifiable, of course. But then her overeating *was* compulsive. Yet it was he who had driven her to fat. Or was it her natural greediness that had driven him away? Fault lay on both sides, surely – and Adam prided himself on being fair.

'Shall we go to the lounge?'

'Yes. Let's.'

Alice led the way to the chintz sofa and cushions and curtains, the carpet of woollen flowers, the prints of the Stag Hunt, and the willow-pattern china behind the mullioned panes of its glass cabinet. There was a disorder in the sitting-room that Adam found new. Alice had always been house-proud. Cleaning had been a god to her. She had been kneeling, ready with brush and pan, while the ash still trembled on the end of his cigarette. Now Peter's toy trains, empty teacups, open magazines, a vanity case, and a powder puff lay on the floor and on the arms of the chairs.

'I'm sorry there's such a mess.'

'That's all right,' Adam said. 'It's a lot for you to do.'

'It just piles up on one.'

Alice sat in a chair and began staring out of the window into the garden, where Peter was swinging upside down from the branch of the specimen apple tree.

'I'd like to give you more money for a help,' Adam said. 'But I can't manage it. The paper's so mean on expenses.'

Alice did not reply. She did not seem to hear. Her body had bent into the stoop that Adam could not bear. She appeared to have fallen forwards under the weight of her breasts, that hung as heavy as the weight at the back of Joyce's head.

'For God's sake, snap out of it, Alice.'

Alice looked at Adam with the stare of a bowl of eggs.

'It's not the end of the world. Must you be so damn sad?'

Alice was still dumb.

'I did my best. It was just so gloomy here. One needs a bit of life.'

'I had a life,' Alice said, 'before I knew you.'

'That was no life, being a solicitor's clerk.'

'It was a life. Now . . .'

The slight movement of her hands in her lap was one which a gardener might use when he pressed the earth tight over a planted bulb.

'That four-girl flat of yours. All squabble and trouble. You were glad to get out of it. You jumped at the chance of getting married and doing nothing.'

'I was sorry for you.'

'Sorry for *me*.' Adam would have liked to laugh. But a sudden stammer stopped his mouth, the stammer of the provincial youth thinking that he was marrying above him. Alice had always been a Londoner. She had known the West End from adolescence. She had been smart and sometimes gay, before the bawdy-talk had given way to baby-talk, and the clothes to plain cooking. While he made his way on Fleet Street, she had regressed in Purley. A wife should be a help to her husband, not a brake on his career. Either develop together or divorce. That was only realistic, and reasonable.

'I was sorry for you,' Alice repeated. 'Such big ideas you had, and nothing to show for them.'

'Nothing? I'm doing all right now.'

'Is Lottie still putting up with you?'

Adam had told Alice of Lottie. His wish to boast had been stronger than his wish to hide.

'I'm still putting up with her.'

'I'd thought I'd fight for you,' Alice said, 'when the time came. But it just wasn't worth it. I made a mistake. That's all.'

'You made a mistake,' Adam agreed magnanimously. 'I wish I could have been a better husband.'

'Could? Couldn't you?'

'It's my nature,' Adam said. Then he added with pride, 'I'm just not satisfied with one woman.'

'You could be, if you tried to be.'

'It's how you're born,' Adam said. 'I was just born oversexed.'

'Lucky for some,' Alice said. Then, off the point, 'The vicar calls every week now.'

'The vulture, you mean. Always pushing his beak into other people's business.'

'Even he doesn't think I can do anything. But I do go to church every Sunday with Peter.'

'Prayer's coming back, they say.' Adam remembered one of Noyes's jokes. 'Modern science confirms that kneeling's the best method of slimming.'

'Don't be cheap,' Alice said. 'You always have to sneer at what you don't understand.'

'I don't need God to lean on. Anyone who can make it on his own two feet . . .'

'If you believed, it wouldn't do you any harm,' Alice said with sudden strength. 'Although I doubt if God would have time for you.'

Adam was surprised by this flash in Alice, almost a bolt of intelligence. Could her faith be making her wise? He smiled at the thought. She was a fool, and not even a holy fool.

'God wouldn't have time for me because he isn't there,' Adam said. 'I'd better be catching the train. That does go at five forty-four precisely. Dead on time. And it doesn't wait for you to catch it.'

'You don't understand,' Alice said. 'You never have. You just live like an animal. Although, who knows, as the vicar said, even a dog may pray.'

'I'd pay two and six to see that,' Adam said, 'at the circus.'

He rose to his feet and began to walk across to the door, where he paused, irresolute.

Alice was sitting straighter now. She stared towards the window, refusing to look at him.

'If there's anything I can do,' Adam said. Alice must need his help.

'Nothing. You've done it already.'

Alice slumped forwards again. The late afternoon light was white grease on her face. Adam stood, and wanted to flee. But he had to justify.

'I've done all I can,' he said. 'You don't realize what it's like to live with you. I'm no saint. But I've stuck it longer than any man could be expected to.'

Alice was dumb.

'You just don't know,' Adam said firmly, 'how to keep a good thing when you've got one.'

He turned and left the house. He stopped to lift the broken trellis into place on the porch. But he had no twine in his pocket. He really would fix it next time, without her asking.

He missed the train by one minute. It was dead on time.

7

'Morgue speaking.'

'Music in my ears. I was beginning to think that the whole world had lost touch with reality.'

'What do you want, Purefoy?'

'I cannot visit Nada today. I have another happy engagement.'

'A funeral?'

'More grotesque, really. A marriage for the sake of a pregnancy. As if a ceremony could excuse two people from the crime of creating a third to suffer with them.'

'I'll be glad to visit Joyce.'

'Do carry with you my condolences on her swift recovery. She must be taking it badly.'

'She's laughing, I should think.'

'Have you noticed, Mr Quince, how at a distance a howl of grief is indistinguishable from a bellow of joy? God gave us only one grimace for pleasure and pain. So our interpretation of an open mouth is rather subjective. You would laugh, I would mop my tears, and another person – concerned with doing good unlike us both – would put a sweet in the mouth.'

'Excuse me. I must get back to my work.'

'The Morgue must always be busy. Please remember, I may call on you. Unofficially, I fear. If only it could be in the normal line of duty, what joy!'

'Goodbye, Purefoy.'

'Goodbye, Mr Quince.'

*　　*　　*

London was cool and clear. A day with a slight wind and mackerel cloud had flicked its broom along gutter and cornice. Even the old buildings had clean edges. There was a definition to the usual uncertainty of the hodgepodge city with its Jacobean and Georgian and Victorian and modern houses and shops, its cheek by jowl of stone and concrete and brick and plastic and glass, its

styles imported from France or Italy or dredged from the Gothic
fortresses of the English mind.

For a moment, Adam saw a purpose in the confusion of London. It was planned, perhaps, to remind people of the layers of
the ages, of their separation and their coexistence. The shock of a
Queen Anne house in the shadow of twenty storeys of functional
cube served to remind the watcher that the past survived to mea-
sure the present. The old was the yardstick of the new. Without
the dead, Adam thought, the living could hardly know how much
more lucky or smart they were.

Joyce was happy to see Adam. And she welcomed the red roses
in his hand as if he had never brought them before.

'The others were just fading. They never opened. I don't know
what they do to the buds. But these. They're all fresh and new. It's
like having my life again. All unlikely and marvellous.'

Adam laughed with joy. He swept the old roses out of their
white vase in one fistful, ignoring the prick of thorns. He dropped
them in a waste-basket, and put the new roses in the vase. He did
not arrange them as carefully as Purefoy had done. He left them
in casual profusion, sprawling as the chaos and plenty of summer
and harvest.

'I wanted to come back alone,' Adam said. 'I don't know why.
Without Purefoy.'

'The Raker. He couldn't come.'

'I know. That's why I came. To fill the gap.'

'You couldn't fill *his* gap. He's strange. You think you're whole,
in one piece. Then he shows you there's a pit inside you, which
was always there, and you wouldn't admit it. A pit. The fear of
dying. Then he tells you how to fill in the pit. Only I never liked
thinking about it. So the pit was just there.'

'He does make a song and dance about it.'

'I know. But he's very sweet. Look, tell me about you. All there
is to know. Now, I'm alive . . . I can't tell you . . . I'm so curious.
About everyone. Each bit of news is a play. It's a holiday abroad.
I'm alive. Can you believe it? I'm alive.'

Joyce was alive. Although her head and body were still strapped
to the frame and weight, her eyes and her mouth ran, hopped and
skipped and jumped, leapt, swung, lip over lip, lid on top of lid,

with the fine lines round the eyes webbing and smoothing quick as cats'-paws of wind on water. Adam could see the light swirling and eddying in the sudden hollows of her face, where the thin bones made rapids of her moving skin.

'Half-dead, and you're alive, aliver than anyone I've seen in all my misspent days.'

'Tell me. Tell me. I *have* to know. All. All.'

Adam told her the story, more true than false, of his life. If the story was of the life that he wished he had lived, the telling made him believe that he had lived so. The good earth, the farmer father fading in the slum, the rich warm mother, the young reporter making good and making a mess of marriage, the loved son, the coming divorce, a new life ready, but for whom? If Adam did not mention his obituaries and Lottie and his worship of Noyes, it was because they were so unimportant in front of this face that seemed to reflect pity and sympathy and admiration, as the story demanded.

'That's a fine life,' Joyce said.

'Won't you tell me yours?'

'No. Not a word. I'm three days old.'

'A big girl for that.'

'I'm a phoenix from the crash. Reborn. Really. I can't tell you, Adam. Since I've known I'd live again . . . I catch every second like a midge. I've seen Death. I *know* him. He's beastly. Nothing. He just makes you want to be. Be anywhere, anyhow. Just be, where he isn't. I hate Death. I was scared of him before. Now I despise him. I loathe him. I'm going to kill *him*, in my mind.'

'I'll help you kill death.'

'You will? You love being alive?'

'When I love the alive.'

'Then let's only know them. Only the alive.' Joyce began to intone a chant. 'Tiredness is death. Sleep is death. Illness is death. Boredom is death.' Her voice rose again. 'But we, we won't be. We'll be alive.'

'When you're better.'

'I'm better now.'

There was a rapping at the door. 'All visitors to leave, please,' the nurse's voice commanded.

Adam rose to go. On the impulse, he put the back of his hand against Joyce's cheek.

'It's warm,' Joyce said. 'Alive. I can feel the blood hum. In your veins. Rub my skin.'

Adam rubbed his fingers up and down her cheek.

'I'm catching it,' Joyce said. 'Life. You're contagious. Rub it in. Hot. Boiling. Ah . . .'

'Tell me. What can I do for you? Anything?'

'Come back.'

'Tomorrow.'

'In my bag, there's a key. To my room, eleven Annandale Gardens. It'll be in a mess, but never mind. Find my red lion by the bed. And my yellow dressing-gown with the green birds. I want to see it hanging on the door here. Like a garden, waiting for me to get in. And my green slippers, with the feathers on.'

'When you see the feathers, won't you want to fly away?'

'Will you let me go? Or catch me?'

'Catch you.'

'No, you won't. Nobody won't. I'll never be caught again.'

A bell rang in the corridor. Adam stopped stroking the hollow of her cheek. He took a key from her white handbag.

'I must go, Joyce,' Adam said. 'I'll bring the lion and the dressing-gown and the slippers.'

'You're a honey.'

'You're a bee. Goodbye.'

*   *   *

Joyce's room was a lost battle to the eye. Sleeves gaped their mouths, demanding hangers. Stockings were twisted in pain, in quest of the splint of a human leg. Jumpers were tumbled on the unmade bed; their mute sprawl cried for a decent laying-out. From open drawers, shirts held out their arms, cut off at the wrist, begging for mercy. Dresses without bodies despaired of their shape and collapsed on chairs. Cups held up their two hollow palms for the charity of breasts. Coats lay abandoned on the carpet, imploring to be taken along with the retreat. Shoes were holed by shrapnel. Discarded brass cases held bullets of lipstick. Cotton wool, smeared with pink, implied the dressing of wounds. And the one object suspended from a hook, clean and dominant, completed the illusion of a battlefield. It was a red jacket and trousers, bright with gold buttons, edged with black piping, military and commanding the room. However bloody the fight, the general must have a change of uniform.

When Adam saw the litter of the room, he felt disgust. He had been trained to feel so. But the love in him worked against his habituation. As he searched among the piles of clothing for the dressing-gown and slippers and red lion, he found himself holding up each article of dress, feeling the nap of cloth and silk and linen, measuring the length of coats against his chest and thigh, smiling over outrageous colours and unnecessary frills. At first, he dropped the clothes where he had found them. But some instinct in him, an urge that he would have despised as feminine before that moment, made him begin to fold and smooth the wrappings of Joyce's life.

Adam spent two hours in the room. He tidied everything. He even wiped off the words, which a lipstick had written on the mirror.

> HAIRDRESS
> BILLS
> GIRDLE HOOK
> RAKER

With a rag, he cleaned the glass on the theatrical prints and photographs on the walls, scenes of Irving and Ellen Terry and George Bernard Shaw. He used a clothes-brush to sweep the floor, and went on his hands and knees to pick up the last pieces of fluff and cotton. Adam was a thorough man.

He left the making of the double bed until the end. The coverlet was green, the sheets purple. There was a hollow on the lower sheet, where Joyce's body had lain. Adam ran his hand round the hollow. He was curiously disappointed to find the sheet cold. He had expected to find it still warm in sympathy with Joyce's rage for life.

Behind him, a key sounded in the lock of the door. Adam stood up from the bed. He turned. Purefoy came into the room. He was carrying several parcels in his hand. They looked at each other. Purefoy seemed to show no surprise on his pale face.

'Well met, Mr Quince.'

'Joyce gave me the key to get some things for her.'

'Please, no justification. I quite understand.'

Adam was immediately angry that he had found it necessary to give a reason for his presence. He would involve Purefoy in a similar self-defence.

'Why are you here?'

'These parcels are so damnably heavy.' Purefoy put down his packages neatly on the chest of drawers. 'I thought I might store them here until I recovered my breath.'

The lie was transparent. Adam demanded a confession.

'You have a key?'

'I normally break in with a crow-bar,' Purefoy said lightly. 'But I stupidly left it behind.'

'Does Joyce know you've got a key?'

'My dear Quince! Do remember, you become the guardian of the lives of others only when they die.'

'I'll tell her I met you here.'

'Please do. Although I would ask you not to mention these poor parcels. She might not like her room serving as a left-luggage counter.'

'I won't mention them.'

Adam was thwarted. He hid his defeat by turning to the bed. He smoothed the sheets and straightened the blankets in a fury of concentration.

'You have a mania for order,' Purefoy said. 'It must be the influence of your trade. All this reduction of the infinite chaos and misery of one human life into three final paragraphs. I much admired your piece on Peter Comachin, incidentally. It outdid the most skilled work of an American undertaker. While he powders and rouges the departed into a semblance of their living selves, you make their lives absolutely unrecognizable.'

'I do the job I'm paid for,' Adam said sharply. 'And I do it well.'

'Superbly. As I told you, Mr Quince, I deeply admire you. You take a life, dedicated to faith and political action, and you expose the truth behind all human effort, that doing anything is bound to be vain and useless and incomprehensible to the rest of mankind. We know not what we do. And if we are known by what we do, we are known wrongly. Your life of Mr Comachin persuaded me even more of the virtue of total inaction. To do nothing is to commit no crime. The need is to suffer oneself, not to pass on suffering. Endure alone, Mr Quince. Do not spread your sorrow on to others. Thank you for reminding me. You are correct, as always.'

Adam did not know how to reply. He had only learned to despise philosophy as a waste of time for those who did not want to work. He could not answer its arguments. Yet all of Purefoy's sentences seemed to have the same damned literary sound. He spoke as if he were delivering a dictation to a class of one, or reading out the last will and testament of an aristocrat waiting for the tumbrils. How could he have avoided contact with all modern slang, and even conversation? His knowledge of the English language had stopped in the days before Adam was born. Adam could not believe that any man could be so out of his own time. It was unnatural. It was an act. And yet, by now, Adam could not conceive of Purefoy acting or speaking in any other way.

Adam gathered up the yellow, silk dressing-gown with its embroidered green peacocks, the emerald slippers with their feathered rims, and the toy red lion with the Union Jack stitched under its tail. He was ready to leave. After a minute, he thought of an answer.

'If I believed you believed one word you said, Purefoy, I could never write another sentence.'

Purefoy, as always, did not have to pause for his reply.

'Of course I cannot believe what I say, Mr Quince. I cannot *believe* anything. That would demand from me far too much sureness of self, one of your most admirable and incredible qualities.'

Purefoy's flattery seemed again to be something of a sneer. It was an appeal to vanity, not to sense.

'Then why do you talk so much?' Adam said.

'Exercise is good for the tongue. Indeed, they say that silence has a bad effect on the nerves. For purely selfish reasons, Mr Quince, I like to talk, if I can find ears to hear.'

'Not mine.' Adam walked over to the door, then paused. 'Why were you called the Raker?' he said.

'An undergraduate nonsense,' Purefoy said. 'Based on a quotation from Daniel Defoe, whom I dote upon. Have you ever dipped into the *Journal of the Plague Year?*'

'I must forget to order it.'

'Seriously, I think you should glance at it. It describes how we should behave each year of our lives. We do not do so, because we need plague or famine or fire or disaster to remind us of our condition. In the Great Plague . . .'

'I just wanted to know why you were called the Raker.'

The white hair of John Purefoy stood above his pallor like the hood of a monk. Even the smoothness of his pale cheeks shone with a skin of ice.

'At the height of the Plague in 1665, the mayor and aldermen of the City of London put out Orders for Cleansing and Keeping of the Streets Swept. One item ran, "It is thought necessary, and so ordered, that the sweeping and filth of houses be daily carried away by the Rakers, and that the Raker shall give notice of his coming by the blowing of a horn, as hitherto hath been done." The Raker shall give notice of his coming by the blowing of a horn, Mr Quince. Perhaps that is why I talk so much.'

PART TWO

The Obituary Man

Unlucky Greeks, are we not dead,
Seeming alive, by dreaming fed?
Or do we live, and is life dead?

PALLADAS OF ALEXANDRIA

8

In the winter, Adam and Joyce became lovers.

They went to Kew Gardens, one January afternoon. Joyce wore a green coat and a yellow shawl wound twice round her neck and over her chin to hide the plaster cast. She leaned on Adam's arm. She was still faint after months in hospital. She had insisted on going to Kew. Even bare trees, she said, made her think of spring. Their branches were the beds of leaves. Green things came from black beginnings.

A cold wind was cutting from the Thames. Once past the entrance wall, they had to lean forwards at the waist as they beat their way towards the first hot-house. Adam felt as if a cold shelf were laid against his left cheek. His trouser-legs beneath his overcoat were slabs along his shins. He supported Joyce with one arm round her waist and one hand under her elbow. The iron and glass fantasy of the first hot-house with its spire and tracery and white envelope, like some airship in a skeletal hangar, could have been a mirage. Its probability receded as the visitors advanced. But, on the sudden, they were there, through the glass door, into the muggy interior.

The warm air was a relief, a relaxation, then a draining of strength, a coming of weakness for Adam. His eyes were swamped by jade and emerald and verdigris, by the green of lawn and mould and marsh. The blades of fronds were caught in the twine of creepers. Plants with teeth like saws threatened to amputate flesh and blood. Trees reared their scaly trunks high as the pillars of iron to where cat-walks made their spreading tops humble as bushes. The gratings on the gangways were wet. An invisible steam coated the surface of glass and leaf. It was a kempt jungle, an Eden on Cancer. All the beasts had been excluded, except for human beings.

'I can breathe here,' Joyce said.

She pulled Adam towards a scarlet and spined flower that protruded across the passage-way.

'I'm stifling,' Adam said.

Sweat was pricking its aquapuncture along Adam's flesh, still cold from the wind outside. His lungs found the swallowing of spears of blast in the gardens preferable to the gulps of wet wool in the hot-house. He felt swaddled by Joyce.

'I need heat,' Joyce said. 'Like this red flower. It makes me bud. Put out petals all over. Feel my skin. Feel it.'

Adam put his palm on Joyce's cheek. He could feel a quickening of her blood, something forcing and moving, the plucking strings of her body.

'I feel it.'

'That's why I wanted to come. All bleak outside. Wind to cut your head clean off. Then in here. Where they've caught the heat. In a glass net. It's the Amazon. Congo. Can't you feel it, Adam? Your skin's the skin on a drum.'

Her fingers were felt hammers in a piano. They tapped the bones and sinews in Adam's hand on her shoulder. Broken rhythms of dry finger-tips. But his skin was moist in the heat, unresponsive.

'I feel them,' he lied.

'Listen. Tip, tapper, tap. Tip, tapper, tap. Mumbo Jumbo, God of the Congo, Mumbo Jumbo, God of the Congo, Mumbo Jumbo will hoodoo you. Think back. When we were all black. Dancing in bare skin when the Thames was on Capricorn. Back further. When we had gills and fins. Flicking our tails to the tides, when the moon pulled them. Back. Back. We're amoebas. The music of the spheres. We're one. Both of us, one, in the first amoeba. Then Venus crosses Saturn. And we split apart. And it all begins. Adam and Eve. Adam and Eve. Listen.'

The tapping of the fingers on the back of Adam's hand quickened. Now it was a running barrage of blows, so fast it was nearly a clawing at his skin. Joyce's eyes were bright. Their amber was blown into a coal. A flush circled her cheek.

Adam tensed his muscles deliberately, infusing artificial excitement. But he could only sense the sweat on him, the steam in the air, the weight of his coat dragging down his shoulders. He swayed from side to side, pretending he had caught the beat of a drum.

'Mumbo Jumbo, God of the Congo,' he intoned.

'In the hot-house here, beginning to end. Alpha to Omega.

Even before. Listen. A sun. Only a great fire. Another sun blazing. A collision. We're shaken off, dust from a furnace. We're coal, whirling round the sun. Then a crust on our earth. A dead crust, only living when we face the sun, our mother fire. All life from the sun. We, condemned to grow cold, yearning for the sun. The sea floods the earth. It is dark, deep, a grave. A grave that shifts and flows, breeding. Then out we crawl, out on to the sand, hot in the sun. And we walk on legs. And we learn to fly, higher, higher. Promise me, Adam . . .'

Her fingers stopped their drumming, clutched, dug down between the bones of Adam's hand.

'Promise you what?'

'If ever we live that long, and it's possible . . . I mean, we'll be on the moon soon . . .'

'Yes. Soon.'

'You'll come with me. We'll take a steel ship. And go. On and through and up. Dive up the dark air, black and deep as the sea. Till it grows hotter, whiter. And the ship melts. And the sun sucks us in. We can't turn back. The pull's too strong. We burn, drawn on. We melt in the sun, fuse, join again. We reach God. Life in death. It would be. Life in death.'

Joyce was shaking now, shuddering in her hope. The heavy atmosphere was pressing Adam's face with hot towels. He put an arm round Joyce's shoulder. She began to sag, a balloon in which the gas grows cold.

'I'll take you home, my dear,' Adam said.

'Yes.'

'I'll take you to the sun one of these days. Majorca.'

'Yes.'

'We'll live on the beach. Suck up the sun through our skins till we're mahogany all over. You'll see.'

'I see. Take me back home.'

When they left the hot-house, the sweat dried on Adam. He shivered in the shreds of wind, sliced by the graters of the branches without leaf on the winter trees. He could feel his own bare bone. Even the water in his blood was chill.

He had to find a taxi for Joyce outside the gate. He put her straight to bed, when they returned to her flat. He gave her lemon tea and aspirin. She slept for three hours. When she woke, she held out her arms to Adam. Her face was quiet, almost resigned, above the plaster cast that made a slave-halter round her neck.

Adam was gentle with her. Later that night they became lovers.

9

ADAM moved into a room in Joyce's house of self-contained flatlets for professional people. He waited until Lottie went away for a week-end, and then he called at her house. As she was not there, he left a note, explaining all to her.

Lottie dearest,

I feel things have come to a climax between us. Our love is too great or too destructive. I need time to think things over. I will go and live by myself for some months. Perhaps we could meet then to decide our future for ever, once my divorce is through. Please do not contact me at the office. This is best for both of us.

My love,

ADAM

He surprised himself in his kindness to Joyce. There was something gawky, underdeveloped in her body that made him treat her as a loved child. Her thinness was pointed by the thick plaster on spine and under chin. Even when the plaster was cut away, muscle had shrunk and skin had bleached to make her neck narrow, starved and separate from shoulder and breast.

Adam brought her fruit and flowers daily, and things to feed her up. He had a winning flutter on the horses, and could afford to be kind. He took her chicken jelly, bananas, beef cubes, grapes, all the restoratives of his youth. Joyce laughed to see his choices, but ate them obediently. She seemed to depend on his care each day. She had little will to go out. It was as if her struggle for survival had exhausted her vitality. And if, at times, Adam seemed only to provoke more listlessness in her, he could put it down to a reaction from her illness.

Yet, from time to time, Joyce's energy returned. Her hands would pluck at Adam's sleeve, let go, pluck an inch higher. Her gestures would hover and dart and fly backwards as quick as hum-ming-birds. Her limbs seemed to have a life of their own, an abso-lute independence of movement. With one bare foot she would pick up a stocking, while she smothered the other foot by sitting on it, upon a stool in front of her dressing-table. Simultaneously, she would be feeling with one hand across the litter in front of her for a powder-puff, while the other hand pushed back her hair from her brow. While these three actions were continuing, her eyes would be staring at the outline of her lips, which would be plumping in and out to spread lipstick evenly over their surfaces. When Adam took Joyce in his arms, it was like holding a sackful of hens. Pieces of struggling cloth would bulge out in all directions. And, every so often, an edge of shoulder-blade or hip-bone or shin as sharp as a beak would peck at the containing Adam.

In normal motion, Joyce's face lost the carved quality of Adam's first impression of her. Her top lip tended to roll upwards like a rabbit's mouth eating an invisible lettuce. Although her face was lean, a white fur on her skin seemed to concentrate and hold the light on her features. From the front, the bridge of her nose was a little broad and flat, the eyes a little round, their amber a little animal. If Joyce did not have the long ears of the rabbit, the fact that her shawl of black hair always hid her cheeks and neck made Adam suspect that she might be concealing her true nature. He was relieved when she put on a head-band to cream her face, and showed two white ears, small and set close to her skull, all too delicate and human.

Adam and Joyce were brought together by being neighbours. His decision to live along the corridor meant months of casual en-counters. He found his own room too bare with its coarse green linen bedspread, an oatmeal carpet, a single corduroy-covered arm-chair, and a gas-meter that ticked out warmth by shillings. So he would drop in continually to visit Joyce, carrying small gifts. And, at once, the clutter of her room would soothe him and make him feel indulgent. He would help her tidy up, gently scolding. And he would only leave her reluctantly, when she insisted.

Adam and Joyce developed between them the private code and games of lovers. The red lion became their keepsake. When his tail flaunted the Union Jack on the shelf above Joyce's bed, Adam was allowed to sleep there. When the lion walked down the corridor, Joyce visited Adam's room. Sometimes the lion even seemed to roar out of his woollen mouth when Adam lost and found himself in Joyce's body, and his blood swelled to a cataract in his ears. They called the lion Borzoi, because he wasn't.

Adam had all the pleasure of having Joyce as his wife without the duty of keeping her. He enjoyed her company and did not pay her bills. She always seemed to have money, and Adam did not ask its source. He feared to know the answer.

Such little things made Adam yearn: –

To watch Joyce come out of the changing-stall in a boutique, wearing a purple dress, while she smiled at him to show him the cleverness of her choice.

To press each peach in a box and test its yielding firmness before buying, because Joyce would gobble it down at once, green or not.

To feel materials after Joyce had run them between her finger and thumb, and try to discover what syrup or thorn made Joyce stick to one and drop another.

To stoop and stroke a fat calico cat sunning itself on their basement step, while Joyce's face grinned and admired his kindness.

To fry a chop on the gas-ring, showering it with spices until the pepper made him sneeze and the final taste made him swear never to cook again.

To knead the muscles of Joyce's thin shoulders after the cast had been removed, and to hear her moan and say, 'Go on, go on,' with the muscles soft as spaghetti under her skin, hardening, hardening, with time.

To know in the dead hours in the Morgue that Joyce would be waiting for his telephone call, forbidden to ring him, and that he would say, 'Mister Welsh,' and she would say, 'Miss Rarebit,' and they would both say, 'Soft Cheese,' before they laughed together in their conspiracy of idiocy and started to chatter.

There was such a delight in so many little things with Joyce that Adam began to sense the texture and the surface of being alive. The skin of his eyes and hand touched the skin of the streets and the shops and the rooms and the parks and the people. The skins were the same skin, the skin of the senses that Nature puts round all her creatures and objects so that they may know one another.

For the first time since he was a child, Adam felt himself no better, no worse, the same as the stuff of the world.

He could learn little of Joyce's past, because she would rarely admit to one. She was not ashamed of her background. She found it irrelevant. When she had first become an actress, she had made a cult of the here and now. She had injected enthusiasm and warmth into her tone. But, after a time, the repeated acting had become the fact of her character. She had also learned that freedom from the dreary and the everyday lay in concentration on the amusing detail. She had once thought, in the infinite wisdom of adolescence, that small things were silly. Later, in the silliness of maturity, she had found out that wondering at the small was her way of weighing the great.

If Adam's method of dealing with the past was through denial of it, Joyce's was through forgetfulness. She did not wish to remember, and so she put her youth out of her mind, like the lines from some part that she had not wanted to play. If someone had said to her that the child was mother to the woman, she would have said that she was an exception to the rule. The old child in her was buried, the woman was a new and larger child. She learned only enough of the way of the world to defend herself against it, when necessary. She would learn no more, in case the world corrupted her. She was clever in knowing that the innocent have to be wary to save themselves, and that flight is the protection of the weak. She would allow others to impose on her until the day she died, for fear of the greater evil of being suspicious of the human race.

In his love of Joyce, Adam did not see that the winter of her content was only a seasonal affair. When the March winds began to huff in scraps of sunshine, he thought that her restlessness was a wish to escape with him, not from him. When she sent him away and spent the night alone, he thought it was because she wished to spare him the sight of her occasional pains. When she complained, 'You're hurting me,' in his arms, he thought it was her illness, not her indifference. When he boasted of his successes in Fleet Street, he thought that her look of vacancy was her dream of their future life together, not her withdrawal from his crassness. When she objected to his vulgarity, he thought that she was secretly praising the dominant male in him, and he became even more masculine and masterful. Adam could not see that Joyce's affection for him was simply because he was present during her convalescence. There was, after all, no one else.

This alone puzzled Adam. He could not understand why Joyce was so isolated. Nobody came to see her, except for the Raker, who called every afternoon while Adam was at work. She had no family, and no friends whom she wished to visit. Adam would have liked to have plucked her as a mistress from a crowd of dashing young actors. He resented his lack of competition, and found it unnatural. So he waited one day until Joyce was in a talking mood, as she dried her dark hair in front of the electric fire.

'It's odd you have no friends,' he said. 'Only your agent, Purefoy and me.'

'It's simple enough. I never needed anybody else when I was with the Raker. He taught me everything. For years.'

'He must have depressed you utterly.'

'Hardly ever, Adam. You don't know what fun he was. I'm an incurable optimist, as you know. I'm impossible to get down. He's a god among pessimists. You can't get him up. So we used to play these games. Think of a word.'

'Stone,' Adam said.

'Catapult.'

'Catapult?'

'Yes, Adam. What do you think of when you hear stone?'

'I don't know. Milestone.'

'Well, the Raker would think of tomb or gall-stone. So we'd laugh. And we'd never think of the same. Except once. When he said, Nada. And we both said, Lily.'

'Nada the Lily. Isn't that a novel by Rider Haggard?'

'She was a very alive, very beautiful black girl. Like me, except only my hair's black. That's why I liked the Raker's name for me, Nada.'

'But he told me it meant Nothingness,' Adam said.

'I always think of the lily. A black lily. So does the Raker. But otherwise, we never got the same answer. Always the opposite. We'd call it the life and death game. He was always on the wrong side.'

'It's a pose of his.'

'No, it's true.' Joyce looked into the burning coils of the fire, and spread her fingers like racks under her hair. 'That's why the Raker scares me now.'

'Do you have to see him every afternoon?' Adam tried to sound disinterested; but jealousy made his voice sharp.

'He can see me any time he likes. He really made me.'

'I bet he made you,' Adam said. 'Every night.'

'You can be so cheap, Adam. I suppose it's just how you have to talk in Fleet Street. But you needn't here.'

'I'm sorry, Joyce.'

'For your information, when the Raker took me to London, he wouldn't touch me. Not till I was settled, had a job, was quite independent. I had to force him into bed with me. It wasn't easy.'

'I don't believe it.'

'He can't stand people's gratitude, you know. That's why, when he gives me presents, he pretends he's too tired to carry a parcel any further. Or he's throwing out a bit of junk, like a new Dior dress, could I possibly find room for it? I did refuse once or twice. And I had to go and rescue the thing from the dustbin.'

'He's rich. He can afford his gestures.'

'The rich are usually mean,' Joyce said. 'They don't make gestures because they know how to count just what it costs. That's why they're rich. The Raker's not that wealthy, anyway. He's just careful with his money. He jokes about being the last gentleman, you know.'

'I know. He does *try* so hard to be.'

Joyce ignored the innuendo in Adam's emphasis.

'He is. I've met other people trying to be gentlemen. They're not. But the Raker's like a monk. Dedicated to his code. He's supporting me now, you know.'

'I'd hoped not.'

'I never know about it. He wouldn't dream of mentioning it to me. I just suddenly find money in my bank account. From an undisclosed source. When I accuse him of it, he just says, "Impossible, it couldn't be me, I'm far too avaricious." But it is him. He's a bit daft. But it's lovely for a girl. You never feel you *have* to give him anything in return. Only exactly what you really want to give at any time.'

Adam searched for the poseur in Purefoy as eagerly as a puppy for the centre of a tin can.

'I'd find it a bit boring,' he said, 'trying to get down to the man himself through all that armour-plate. There may be nothing underneath, you know. Scratch his surface, and all you'll find is more surface.'

'I didn't live with him long, Adam. We separated, and I came here. You know why I went? It was what you said. You can see a man you respect and admire, would die for, every day. But you can't go on sleeping with someone who stays out of reach. The Raker won't get close to you. He says he doesn't want to hurt you. But he hurts you more by staying away. I cried. I wouldn't see him for months. Then we went back to seeing each other all the time. As friends. He'd get me after the theatre every night, give me dinner. I couldn't live without him.'

'Till the crash,' Adam said.

'Till the crash. I liked cars, you know. Really fast ones. I probably still do. But I won't drive again now. The Raker taught me one thing. If you can't live with Death near all the time, don't go near him. I'd always see him in the driving-mirror.'

'I'm glad it was me you came to, Joyce.'

'I'm glad too,' Joyce said. Her voice was sad.

'I came to the Clinic quite by accident. I was sorry for you.'

'It was nice having someone sorry for me. I was really grateful. I must say, the Raker, I hated him a bit then.'

'He was so bloody about you dying. As if it were lucky for you.'

Joyce shook her head slowly, but only to dry her hair.

'I know. I couldn't take it. Though I should have expected it from the Raker. Somehow, all his talk about death had been a joke. Till it was my own death. And he was *consistent*. Even about *me* dying. When he's so kind and gentle by nature. Yet then, he had to be brutal. It was incredible. To talk like that about someone you love.'

'He loves you?'

'Yes,' Joyce said simply. 'Didn't you know?'

'What about you and me? Doesn't he . . . ?'

'He never mentions you,' Joyce said. 'By his code, you're my private affair.'

Adam felt a spurt of rage against Purefoy. He would not be ignored so easily. He was Joyce's lover, and Purefoy should recognize his position. It gave him rights, importance, status.

'You mean, he's too proud to show how much he cares,' Adam said. 'I bet it really screws him up to think I'm your lover. He's dying to know all the details. It's only natural.'

'No, Adam. For him, you are my private affair.'

Adam bent forwards and kissed Joyce on the mouth. Her drying hair was grass to his face. He felt reassured in this gesture of possession.

'You're so normal, Adam. So like a man when he's as much and no more than a man. If you rolled away all the skins men put on themselves to seem better than they are, there'd be you. The *original* Adam. That's what the Raker calls you.'

'He doesn't mean it your way.'

'He doesn't mean much my way now. He makes me afraid a bit. We don't laugh any more. You see, I *know* about dying. I've seen Death. So when the Raker talks about him, he's there for me. *Here.*'

There was a sudden smell of burning hair in the room. Joyce moved her head back from the fire.

'That's why I like you, Adam. You don't ever think of dying. You just are. You just do. What is it you do, incidentally? I can't ever seem to find out.'

And Adam told her again that he worked on the Racing Page.

10

THE face was its own death-mask. It had no colour. The closed lids were bald eyes. The hair was still wet as clay. It had been brushed into a black hood round the sunk cheeks. The lips had been pressed together. They were blue. The face had a wry look. The girl seemed to be mocking at her own drowning in the Thames. At the last breath, she had twisted her mouth to find that dying was the same as living. The jump from the black bridge to the black fathom deep had meant no river change to her.

A green plastic macintosh covered her body. Her two white feet protruded, two fish on the marble slab. A yellow shoe was attached by its strap to one ankle. The label on the shoe was legible, DOLCIS.

'Any identification?' he said.

'None. You don't recognize her?' the policeman said.

'No. I checked through some possibilities in the files.'

'We thought you might know. You might have been able to help.'

'We'll give her a paragraph. Maybe a photograph too. She's beautiful, you know.'

'Makes you think,' the policeman said, 'what drives them to it.'

'Doesn't it?' Adam said. 'I'll have a photographer sent down. We might feature her. Make something of her like the Inconnue de la Seine.'

'Who was he?'

'A beautiful unknown girl drowned in the Seine in Paris. They made a mask of her face. It became very famous. You can still buy a copy. Our editor's got one. Perhaps we could do the same for her. The Mermaid of the Thames.'

'It won't help her much,' the policeman said.

'Don't you want her identified?'

'The parents always have to know. You have to tell them. If she put an end to it all, she didn't want to make us suffer for her. It's better nobody knows who she is.'

Adam looked at the policeman. His heavy moustache gave him

an air of gravity. His words rolled out from below a thundercloud. They were pronouncements.

Adam turned towards the drowned girl. She was dead. Her certificate said so. But why? Joyce had been as unmoving when he first saw her on her own slab of sheet and frame. That was her luck, to keep her soul.

'I'm going,' Adam said. 'Thanks for asking me down.'

'It's a pleasure,' the policeman said.

*   *   *

Noyes had invited Adam to lunch. They sat in a City chophouse, eating steaks and baked potatoes. They drank Beaujolais by the glass. The fumed oak alcove round their seats had been recently blackened and polished to give it the patina of antiquity. The brass carriage-lamps that lit the table had never travelled further than the length of a modern conveyor-belt, and the distance from factory to restaurant in a carton. The waitresses, dressed in white frilly shirts and floor-long black dresses, were the most convincing part of the decorations. They could have been Dickensian housekeepers, judging by the venom of their voices, shouting orders below stairs.

'How was your morning among the stiffs?' Noyes said. 'Did you shake hands with a friend here and there?'

'There was a very beautiful dead girl. Unknown.'

'You sound quite touched, Quince. I mean, headwise. What's this budding necrophilia of yours? They'll have to be putting up blocks and tackles at the edge of graves soon. To drag you up from your final embrace with the dear departed.'

Adam looked across the table at Noyes's face. Lights flashed on and off in his glass eye. The wires that operated his mouth pulled and jerked. The glib chatter dropped out in a jackpot of pennies.

'You're a one-eyed bandit, Noyes. A Fleet Street fruit machine.'

'Feed me sixpences of slop, and I'll pay you dividends of wisdom. Sentimentality, Quince, is the death of the journalist. We ladle it out, true. But in measured doses. Not a dollop too much. We're chemists. Whoever heard of a chemist taking an overdose? We *sell* the stuff, Quince. We don't drink it. You're going sloppy. You're poisoned. You need a change.'

'Then let me out of the Morgue. Or I'll damn well resign.'

Noyes laughed.

'The day you resign, Quince, the heavens will split their sides. Our Father will die laughing.' Noyes suddenly dropped his banter and put on his wheedle. 'The Chief needs *you*, Quince. Will you obey the call? The Chief expects . . .'

'I'm going,' Adam said, 'unless I get a move.'

'What'll you live on? As you know, anyone who's worked for us becomes one of the gods, not fit to work elsewhere. Or as our rivals say, one of the untouchables. Still, for lepers, we eat damn well.'

'There are other papers.'

'Not for you. We are the one and only. Britain's biggest daily to be. You're on the wagon, so why jump off?'

'I'm going.'

'We'll black you. Up and down the Street. Quince is a has-been before he's started. He couldn't take the Morgue. He's soft, rotten, slack. He can't look a rigor mortis in the eye.'

'Can you, Noyes?'

'Look, I've seen Alamein. D-Day. Belsen. Stiffs high as pyramids. In all shapes and sizes. Some only half-stiff, wishing they were more so.' Noyes put his last piece of rare steak in his mouth, and began mopping up the red gravy with a piece of garlic bread. 'You've seen nothing, Quince. I've seen it all. It's that Lazarus kid of yours. That actress. Back from the edge of the big drop, only to drop in your lap. She's given you spooks.'

'Lay off her.'

'You don't. You lay on her.'

'I said, lay off, Noyes.'

'You're soft on her. You must be. Leaving that bankroll of yours for a kid. Broken neck, huh? Don't break my heart.'

Adam looked at Noyes. He saw the lines round the mouth and nose that he had thought were the true grain of experience. Now they looked like the leavings of envy. Or of mere petulance.

'Just because you couldn't keep any of your own three wives . . .'

'Keep them?' Noyes howled, so that the whole chop-house stiffened to attention. 'Jesus, the trouble with a woman is twisting her arm enough to stop her throttling you. Three wives, when one proves you're a moron. Now, I'm strictly for the pros. Pay for what you get. Anything else is just parsley on a leg of pork. You don't need it, up goes the price, and it mucks up the meat.'

'Have a look in a mirror one day, Noyes. Then don't ask why all your three wives left, crossing themselves with both hands.'

'You're getting uppity, Quince. Don't look now, but I may bust you.' Noyes's glass eye wavered like a warning light.

'I won't. But you won't. You'd get bored not having me to kick around.'

'We could put you on night call. That might cramp your sex a bit.'

'She's resting, being an actress. All the time. Day and night.'

'How about a trip to the Solomon Islands, then? To report on the mating customs of the savages.'

'I'll quit, Noyes. I told you.'

Noyes leaned forwards across the table. He spoke softly.

'You poor sap-head. You believe yourself. That's the beginning of the end.' He took his spare knife and fork, and laid them across each other in front of Adam. 'Pick up your cross and walk, Quince. All down the Street, knocking at every door. See if anyone lets you in. They won't, because, unlike me, they don't run on faith, hope, and charity to bums. If you're not back in the Morgue by five on the dot, you're fired. If you are back, you're on stiffs till the day you die. It'll be my own personal pleasure to hammer another nail in your coffin-lid every time I catch you coming up for air.'

* * *

At one minute to five o'clock, Adam sat in the Morgue. Noyes was right. Noyes was always right. Of course, newspapers were folding. Of course, there were too many journalists out of work. But a man of his ability, drive, future . . . He hadn't got the by-lines, so he couldn't find another job. Noyes had seen to that. They had kept him under, until he could never escape them. They had kept him under, until he was drowned dead, with the files of the living dead as green as mould or weed about him. They had laid him out on a slab of desk, waiting for identification.

'May I intrude?'

Adam turned to see Purefoy standing politely in the open door.

A white lily was in the buttonhole of his pearl-grey suit.

'Please do,' Adam said. 'I'm in a mood for wasting my time.'

'I called earlier. But your charming editor, Mr Noyes, told me that you were absent. He was certain, however, that you would return before five. So I decided to wait.'

'Noyes knew I'd be back?'

'Why? Did you think of staying away?'

'I was always coming back. What do you want, Purefoy?'

'You said once that I might have the honour of seeing the Morgue. I thought that now was the time to take you at your word.'

'Here it is.'

Purefoy looked round the green cabinets that walled the room. He walked forwards to the file marked PON–QUO. He pulled out the tin drawer, and began turning the envelopes.

'Don't touch,' Adam said.

'Excuse my simple curiosity. I was searching for myself.'

'You're not there. We don't know of you. There's nothing on you.'

'So when I die,' Purefoy said, 'you will be unemployed.'

'Yes.'

'Then my end, as I had always hoped, will be as my life, useless to anyone.'

'Yes.'

'Nature, you know, cares only for the species, never for the individual. You, as a perfect human being, Mr Quince, care for the individual and not for the species. I must say, I am on Nature's side. I would rather die insignificant among mankind, no more than an erect ape with a detachable thumb, and no less.'

'Sometimes unknown deaths make the front page,' Adam said. 'There's the Unknown Soldier. And there was a beautiful girl drowned herself today. She looked like . . . like a Greek statue . . .'

'Do you often see your victims personally, Mr Quince?'

'I saw Joyce.'

'Ah, yes. Nada. I came to say . . .'

'This girl was so lovely. Such a damn shame. She could have been a movie star.'

'That would, indeed, have been a fate worse than death. Thus a happier fate.'

Adam felt a rash of rage at this elegant mocker.

'I tell you, Purefoy, it was a bloody shame. There's no need to sneer at her. She can't answer back.'

'I thought this was a mere trade to you, Mr Quince. It earned your pay.'

'I can feel, can't I? I'm not run by the pennies they feed me. I'm not a slot machine. I've got a heart. And when I saw this drowned girl, and I thought of how nearly it might have been Joyce . . .'

'Death seems to be bothering you,' Purefoy said. 'You really should begin to treat him like the old acquaintance which he is. Someone you would be delighted to meet at any time. Formally, of course.'

'You can talk. You haven't a bloody clue what death means. You're just a phoney, Purefoy. A damn phoney.'

'I seem to have interrupted you, Mr Quince, in a moment of despair. I fear I really do intrude. I just wished to say that Nada asked me to inform you that she is going away to the country for a few days.'

'Why didn't she tell me?'

'She only made her arrangements this afternoon.'

'Who's paying? Are you?'

Adam needed to hurt Purefoy in his own hurt. He wanted to make the flesh in front of him wince for the flesh that was going from him.

'Nada is staying with a friend of mine near Chichester,' Purefoy said.

'You made her go.'

'She accepted my invitation. She asked you not to worry. She said she would return soon.'

'You're jealous of me, aren't you, Purefoy? You'd do anything to break us up. I'm sleeping with Joyce. You want to, don't you? You can't stand losing her. But you won't manage it, with all your tricks and graces.'

'Your affairs, Mr Quince, are your affairs,' Purefoy said coldly. 'I do not wish to know of them. If you will excuse me.'

He turned to go. He seemed to pose against the panels of the door, as he had against the door of Joyce's hospital room during the first interview with Adam. He stood erect, his arms hanging by his sides, pallid, smooth-shaven, his white hair brushed into its youthful peak. He could have replaced a dummy, except that his ease with himself gave him an air of relaxation. Adam had once thought this mastery of self and movement to be a pretension in Purefoy. Now its continual and precise repetition led to its recognition by Adam. Purefoy was different from other men because he never betrayed himself. He did not commit the careless actions of the rest of the world. If Purefoy had suddenly scratched his nose now, Adam would have considered him an imposter.

Purefoy moved his hand enough to open the door. And Adam blurted out the question which he had been burning to ask since Purefoy's entrance.

'What the hell are you wearing a white lily for?'

'That? White, the colour of nothingness, of mourning among the Chinese, the wisest of all people. And a lily of the field? They toil not, neither do they spin, Mr Quince. It is *my* flower.'

Adam's voice was a cry.

'You're wearing it for Joyce. Nada the Lily.'

'Only for myself.' Purefoy stood very straight, as though in judgment. 'You and I are the same breed, Mr Quince. We only wear what suits ourselves.'

II

THE snakes were tangled in an undergrowth of love. Behind their glass, they clung together as the limbs of an orgy. The voyeur could not unravel their knots, granny from sailor from splice. The single sleek leg of each serpent was twined ten times over in an interminable embrace. Every scale glinted with a kind of sweat. Adam could not bear the sight, now Joyce was away, and Peter by his side.

'I'll show you the crocodiles.'

The crocodiles were rolls of bark on their sand-pits. One moved its ridge of brow above the level of the pool, evil as any submerged thing with an eye is evil. It came to a shelf of stone, and waded ashore on splayed fat legs. It yawned. Its teeth were beds of nails.

'If a crocodile catches you,' Adam said, 'you have to relax between its jaws. Then it'll store you in its larder under a mudbank. And when it's gone, you can swim up and get away.'

'It'd bite off your leg,' Peter said.

'No. They grip gently. Like this.'

Adam caught Peter's narrow bicep between his finger and thumb, and pinched. He must have pressed too hard, because Peter wriggled and yelped. An old woman behind them, formidable in grey silk coat and high-button shoes, tapped Adam sharply on the side of his neck with her umbrella.

'Stop hurting the boy.'

'He's my son.'

'All the more reason to be ashamed of yourself.' The old woman was sure of her ground. 'People like you shouldn't be allowed to have children.'

She turned and walked away. Peter stuck out his tongue after her, and Adam did not reprove him.

The giraffes were unlikely and toy-like, until their long blue tongues struck like mambas out of their hanging upper lips. The elephants carefully chose between peanuts and pennies and the hands of children. They ate the first, they gave the second to their keepers, they discarded the third. The giant panda sat on its hind legs, cramming bamboo shoots into its mouth with its front paws; its coat was a quilt of fur, too perfect to have been left to the haphazard stitching of Nature. Inferior capybaras grovelled near by in their earth enclosures, woolly lumps with legs, ridiculous objects hoping to pass themselves off as beasts.

'What animal would you like to be?' Peter said.

'A human being,' Adam said.

'He's not an *animal*.'

'He is. He's the most superior of animals.'

'The lion is.'

'It can't think.'

'Yes, he can,' Peter said. 'He can catch things. He's king of the beasts. That's why England is a lion.'

'England, king of the *beasts*? That's not very patriotic.'

'I didn't mean *that*, Father.'

Adam enjoyed the boy's confusion. He remembered how sarcasm or irony had been as bad as the birch to his schooldays. Then, an insult had been a challenge, while adult wit had been a humiliation. Now that he was grown himself, he realized that words were the best weapons against children. To them, words are real. When words are chanted, they become incantations. It took working with words in an adult job to realize that they had little meaning.

In the lion-house of the zoo, the reek of cat limed the nostril. A silent semicircle of watchers was gathered round one cage. Adam joined the arc of crowd. A lion was rearing over a lioness. As he drove down the weight of his flanks upon her, ripping at her back with his foreclaws, she snarled and struck back at him. He shuddered, slipped to the floor of the cage. She struck at him again. He ignored her. She curved her spine, dropping her head. He swung to look at the crowd. Then he roared. Once, twice, three times, four times, he roared. Each new roar caught up the echoes, so that noise rapped continuous at the drums of the ears.

In the cages by the side of the roaring lion's, the other cats ran up and down, leopard and cheetah and ocelot, occasionally mewing. The lion's challenge was reverberate and unanswered. The lioness leaned against his flank, weak.

In the adjoining cage, an old lion, with white spume on his

mane, moved towards the barrier between the cages. The roaring lion turned, scenting a threat. He challenged again. The old lion crouched as if to spring at the barrier. But suddenly, foolishly, he tucked his snout down between his shoulders. Retching made a bellows of his ribs. Bright green vomit streamed in a sheet from his jaws.

'You shouldn't be watching this,' Adam said sharply to Peter.

He pulled the boy roughly by the hand. They left the zoo directly. Adam bought an evening newspaper and read the stale items of the day all the way in the stopping train to Purley. Peter amused himself by blowing up his cheeks and popping them with a forefinger stuck quickly between his lips. In the end, Adam smacked the boy's bare knee, and Peter cried.

*   *   *

When Adam came into the sitting-room of his old house and found the Vicar sitting there with his wife, he suspected a trap. He would be threatened with a pit full of pointed stakes for adulterers. He wanted to turn and run, but good manners kept a smile on his face.

'How nice to see you, Mr . . .'

'Father James,' the Vicar said. 'I think Father sounds so much more apt than Reverend, or Vicar.'

'Do you think old parishioners of ninety like calling you Father?'

'We are all the sons of God, whom I represent in my own poor way.'

Adam could not think of a reply. Alice rose quickly, saying, 'Pardon me, please. I must look at the dinner.' Adam noticed with a shock, as she walked from the room, that she had lost weight. She was no longer fat, merely plump. In the three months that Adam had not seen her because of his affair with Joyce, she had lost twenty pounds. Adam felt his usual guilt. Once he had driven her to fat. Now his worry was that he was driving her to starvation.

'I shall not be staying to dinner,' the Vicar said, soothing Adam.

'Please do.'

'I have other calls,' the Vicar said.

Adam immediately stiffened at the insinuation that he was a case to be visited. 'You sound like a doctor.'

'Souls have diseases,' the Vicar said.

Adam looked at the Vicar's narrow eyes behind their square spectacles. His short bristle of hair, set above jug-handle ears and cheek-bones sharp as knuckles, did give him the look of an ascetic or a pugilist. He would wrestle against Satan. His two hands were not so much folded in his lap as clasped against each other to prevent his fists from flying up into punches. Adam felt in a corner, with the ropes against his back.

'Maybe,' Adam admitted. 'But give me penicillin rather than prayer.'

'Both are necessary.' The Vicar brought up a clenched hand, with its thumb working nervously against the fingers to keep them under control. 'Will you allow me, Mr Quince, to talk a little about you and your wife?'

'If you insist.'

'She is a very good woman.'

'Too good for me,' Adam said.

'That's an easy way out. We are never too good for each other. We can hope that our example will enable others to better themselves. It should not drive them away.'

'Look,' Adam said, 'Alice and I have grown apart. It's not that one of us is better or worse. We're just different. That's all.'

'Good and evil aren't just different. Evil is the enemy of good.'

'I'm not evil,' Adam said, 'and you know it.'

'Of course you're not. How proud you'd be if you were capable of real evil. All you need is to come back to your wife, and try . . .'

'I've tried, Vicar . . .'

'Father James.'

'Vicar. I've tried. It's no use. No good. We make each other sad.'

Adam wanted to remain silent in front of the Vicar. Why should he explain himself to this false judge? But he explained. 'She depressed me. All the time. It's not right to be made miserable all the time.'

'You have not tried, my son. Not with all your heart. You were trying to justify what your selfishness led you to do. Your wife is a good woman, and you have deserted her and your son.'

'You've no right to judge me,' Adam said.

'I am a man of God,' the Vicar said.

'I don't believe in God.'

'Were you baptized? Confirmed?'

'Yes. Before I had any sense.'

'Before you had much sin, you mean.'

'Before I had any sense.'

'Do you, in your arrogance, think that a whole church with millions of communicants can be wrong?'

'Argument by number,' Adam said. 'Why should an error that lasts become a virtue?'

'Have you thought of Creation? Of its infinite complexity, beyond the grasp of man?' The Vicar now leaned forwards, with both fists raised in front of his shoulders, seeming about to strike.

'Argument by our ignorance. We're getting smarter every day.' Adam brought up a hand under his chin to scratch his throat. He kept it there, in case of the need for self-defence.

'What of evil? How could we bear to live without Someone to grant us grace and forgiveness, to make us better than we are by nature?'

'Argument by nonsense. It's a bum deal, the world, Vicar. God's the only excuse that saves the weak from the strong.'

'Your mind cannot even comprehend the universe. It is a pitiful thing. Somewhere, there is a Mind who understands you and all of the human race. There must be, or there would be no community in humanity. No common spirit.'

'Argument by spirit. Show me a soul, Vicar, and I'll be your convert any old time.'

The Vicar brought down a fist on the arm of the chintz-covered chair. The cloth muffled the sound of the blow, but the frame of the chair groaned.

'Three thousand years of belief, billions baptized and dying in the faith, and *you* deny it all.'

'Argument by history, when history is bunk. I don't want to know why so many people were fools before us.'

'And death,' the Vicar said. 'How can you bear the thought of death? Do you end down there in a rotten coffin? Or do you go to a hereafter? Another life? Through the love and grace of God.'

Adam felt a pluck of fear, as he always felt when anyone talked seriously of death. He did not like its fact mentioned. If he did not believe that he would live for ever, he hated to be reminded that he must die.

'Argument by false hope,' Adam said, with a brave face. 'I croak, and I finish. If the fish don't get me, the worms must. So what? I'll live all the life I've got to live. And enjoy it.'

'Even when you die, God won't let you die. He alone knows what you have done.' The Vicar's voice was thick with threat. 'Man can never know what he himself has committed. Only God, and He will judge you.'

'Argument by terror,' Adam said, and managed a careful yawn.

'You have all the answers,' the Vicar said. 'But you have never asked yourself one question.'

'What's that?'

'Your pigeon-holes against real thought. Your Arguments By. Aren't they arguments against argument?'

'I can argue all right.'

'No, you cannot. If you have ears to hear, you may hear. But you are selfish, Mr Quince. You are deaf. You only listen to arguments which prove your own prejudices.'

The Vicar rose. He stood over Adam, his fists hanging in front of Adam's nose. Adam could see the veins twisting up to the red knuckles. He felt a pain between his eyes, in anticipation of the hammer of the Lord.

'That's what we all do,' Adam countered bravely. 'Just speak up for our own prejudices.'

'I will not continue,' the Vicar said. 'I shall advise your wife to leave you. Begin a new life. I have never given this advice to any Christian before. But in your case, I find heresy. Rank heresy. The heresy of indifference, which is worse than the heresy of disbelief.'

'I'm a genuine agnostic,' Adam protested.

The Vicar walked towards the door, where he turned. He held up one fist, then he dropped it again. His voice was almost brutal.

'There's nothing genuine in you,' he said. 'You shame the name of agnostic. For you have no values, human or otherwise. You are a thing of our time, Mr Quince. A creature of circumstance. And God can have no mercy on your soul, until you discover what a human soul is.'

The Vicar left the room in a scurry of cassock. Adam heard the grandfather clock in the hall begin to strike. Above the chimes, the Vicar called out, 'Good evening, Mrs Quince. Please see me after matins on Sunday.' And Adam heard Alice's reply, 'Yes, Father, and thank you.' Then the noise of the front door closing made an eighth knock to the seven chimes of the hour.

Alice came into the room. She wiped her hands on her apron, then pushed her hair backwards behind her ears.

'Dinner's ready,' she said, 'in a few minutes. You can start on the soup.'

'That bloody vulture,' Adam said. 'Poking his priestly nose into our business.'

'You've said that before,' Alice said. 'And you were wrong the first time. Father's been a great help to me.'

With this remark, Adam knew that he would do nothing to stop the divorce becoming final. Between him and Alice was the gulf between man and God. He could not live with the fact of worship about him. He must put the divine out of his mind. Of course God did not exist; but He certainly made enough trouble for those who knew He did not.

12

SPRING was late in London. The people, sapped by a wet and cold winter, were suffering from mild diseases. Working hours were spent in no-man's-land. The streets became trenches. Volleys of coughs crackled everywhere, irregular as snipers. Noses exploded in handkerchiefs with the noise of mortars. Occasionally the heavy battery of a cleared throat grumbled. The commuters huddled deep into overcoats and scarves against the rain and the wind. They were waiting for the zero hour of spring, either the final assault before the sun or an armistice of greenery.

Adam had a cold himself. He felt the pressure of two hot thumbs between his eyes, the warning of his old sinus complaint. Tears trickled unbidden down his cheeks, and his nose dribbled down his sore upper lip. He cursed the weather, his job, Joyce's absence, Joyce's silence, the buses, the rest of mankind, everyone except himself.

A note from Noyes was waiting on Adam's desk. It demanded his presence in the editor's office immediately. It was handwritten. The usual crabbed script wavered as if it had been scribbled in a high wind.

When Adam entered Noyes's office with its large double window overlooking Fleet Street, he noticed two peculiarities. The chair of Noyes's secretary was empty, and Noyes was a man who could not bear a minute of existence without an audience in his pay and power. And secondly, Noyes himself held his head sunk in his hands in a melodramatic posture of despair.

'It's yours truly,' Adam said.

Noyes did not raise his head.

'Sit down,' he whispered between his hands.

Adam sat on a swing chair, made in squares of genuine black leather. He took out his cigarette-case and snapped it open. 'Turkish or Virginian,' he said.

Noyes dragged up a terrible cough from his lower belly.

'Put them away,' he croaked. 'Don't smoke in here.'

Adam had already put a Virginian cigarette between his lips. He removed it, surprised.

'Since when was this a non-smoker?'

'Since today,' Noyes said. His face appeared between his hands. He looked as if he were three days drowned, puffy, white, with one eye red and one glassy.

'O.K., Small Chief,' Adam said. He put the cigarette back under its band, although he had already moistened it on his lip. 'Don't tell me life's so good you want to live longer.'

'Live longer?'

'Or are cancer-sticks just out because your biting tooth's turned sweet?'

'You're fired,' Noyes said.

'What for?'

'For being a fool. And worse. A screwer of your friends. A bloody gloater. You're a hyena. You can only laugh at a carcass.'

After his brief show of usual venom, Noyes had a relapse. His head sank between his hands again.

'I'm really fired?' Adam said in wonder. The first ache in his bowels gave way to a curious rising sensation, a bubble in his gut. Could it be joy? If the decision had been taken out of his hands, it might prove the escape for him, which he was too weak to take.

'You monster,' Noyes groaned, as if seeking pity.

'What sort of compensation will I get? Two-fifty quid?' Adam bid as high as he dared.

'You *are* a monster. You'll get nothing.'

'I damn well will.'

'All you think of is money. Money! When your friends are at death's door.'

'I've got to live,' Adam said defensively.

Noyes dropped his hands. He looked tragically across the desk. His glass eye was round in his face, his real eye almost closed. Instead of an air of profound melancholy, all he achieved was a lecherous wink.

'I've got to die,' Noyes said. His voice was a sentence of death in itself.

'We've all got to go,' Adam said brightly.

'I mean it, you fool. I'm dying soon.'

Adam looked at Noyes. He began to be aware that the old devil was serious.

'What's wrong with you? 'Flu?'

'I've got a tumour in my throat. They took the X-ray yesterday. They'll tell me this afternoon.'

'Cancer?'

Noyes nodded mutely.

As Adam spoke the word cancer, he closed his eyes. Behind his lids, he saw a succession of black crab claws pulping small circles of red into blotches that spilled away into nothing. The skin of his whole body seemed to flake inside. As if in a moment of vision, he could see the exposed sinews of nerves and veins and vessels of his body, the pipes of his blood and will, carrying the red corpuscles into the jaws of the white, renewing the food of the moderate cancer that eats all living things in the name of regeneration and change and age. He shivered. The word cancer had shown Adam the horror of daily death.

'Stop,' Adam sighed. 'Please stop.'

'What's that?' Noyes was offended.

'I'm sorry. I was thinking.'

'That's a change.'

'I'm sorry for you,' Adam said. 'But it's not definite yet.'

'As near as makes no odds. Come here.'

Adam approached the desk, treading softly as if at a bed-side.

'Give me your hand.'

Noyes took Adam's hand in his. Adam's hand recoiled, then let itself be grasped. He could feel the heat and jump of Noyes's flesh. His palm was placed against the side of Noyes's neck. Some vein beat as a pulse.

'Feel. Can you feel it?'

Adam's finger-tips roughed against the bristle of Noyes's wind-pipe. As Noyes swallowed, a ridge of muscle jiggered up and down.

'Press down. You'll feel it then.'

As Adam pressed, he sensed a lump beneath the skin that rolled sideways beneath his touch.

'I feel it,' he said. He took his hand back swiftly, as though the lump were contagious. Automatically, he wiped his fingers on the side of his trousers. Perhaps the plague had stuck to him.

'I'm going to die,' Noyes whispered.

Adam looked down at the thin hair, creamed in separate black threads across the pasty scalp. He pitied Noyes. There, he said to himself, but for the grace of God, go I. And he shivered again, feeling sudden warnings of pain, where no pain was.

'It's not certain, old man,' he said. 'It might just be a cyst. Or an abscess.'

'It's cancer. I know it in my blood.' Noyes put his hand under his chin. 'I've had a premonition. I've woken up choking for nearly a month. As though I had a noose round my neck.'

Adam tried a joke.

'I'll buy you a black hood for your head. So you can't see the drop when you go.'

'It's no joke,' Noyes screamed. 'You wait till your number's up.'

All over Adam's skin, the pores pricked. He was made of lightbulb glass. At a tap, he would disintegrate.

'Are you going to retire, Noyes? Have a last fling?'

'What's the use?' Noyes looked out of the picture window that cut off all noise from Fleet Street by means of its double panes. Adam followed his stare down to the two lines of people walking in opposite directions, indifferent to one another, occasionally jostling or avoiding contact. No one greeted another, nor stopped to stare at a window. There was not even a badger under the wheels of a bus to attract attention from an errand or a meal.

'Nothing matters now,' Noyes said flatly. 'I thought I was doing something in this job. But even the paper doesn't matter. The Chief can go stuff himself.'

'What'll you do?'

'I don't know. Walk so far inland that people think the ink on my fingers is manure, and drink myself blind.'

'I'll have to find a job too.'

Noyes looked at Adam with hate.

'You'll get a job. You're alive. Alive. Just to live, I'd be a crossing-sweeper.'

Adam stared down at Noyes. The dying man was scabby in his desperate grasp on his life. He was a crossing-sweeper already. Cleaning the roads between the Chief and his exploited workers. Sweeping the garbage into the gutters so that the lines of communication were brutal and efficient. A lickspittle hireling with a will that he could only call someone else's.

'I'll get back to the Morgue,' Adam said contemptuously. 'I'd better check your file. It's the last thing I can do for you, old man, to get your obit in order before I clear my own things out.'

Noyes looked speechlessly at Adam. His mouth opened to shout, but a cough strangled him. He put both hands on his throat. His head shuddered. Adam turned towards the door. As he walked away, his own sinus burned in his forehead. He took out his handkerchief. When the office door was closed behind him, he blew his nose. Hot tongs grabbed his brow. Tears ran from the corners of his eyes, tears that Noyes might have mistaken for grief. The pain of Adam's cold hurt him more than the knowledge that Noyes must die soon.

⋆　⋆　⋆

On the top of his desk, Adam made a pyramid of his possessions from the drawers. An indiarubber, elastic bands, a bottle of blue-black ink, some personal writing paper, envelopes to match by courtesy of the newspaper, postage stamps, thirteen empty ball-point pens, seventeen unsharpened pencils of various colours, one conch shell as an ornament, and seven paper-clips in mint and silver condition. Adam intended to make a clean sweep of his going. He would leave the Chief nothing.

In his happiness and relief at his escape, Adam began to sing to himself. He was tone-deaf, and had no voice. Yet the garbled tunes that came out of his mouth were more joyous than choirs of praise. They were the tuneless music of a new man, bawling his pleasure at being born again.

Two telephone calls changed Adam's plans. In the delight of his escape from his burrow, he had become careless. When the telephone rang, he did not wait to check on the caller. He spoke without thought, happily.

'Morgue speaking.'

'Could I speak to Adam Quince?' a woman said.

'That's me. Morgue speaking. The very last speech from beyond the tomb. You're in luck.' Adam did not recognize the voice in the distortion of the receiver. It was sure to be someone's secretary.

Stenographers, unlike their employers, seemed to have no trouble in finding jobs.

'Adam. This is Joyce.'

Again the pit yawned in Adam's bowels. His joy drained away into a sump within him. In his head his sinus was a fiery reminder of mortality.

'Oh, Joyce. Hello.'

'I'm sorry to disturb you at work. I'm passing through London tomorrow on my way to Manchester. I've been offered a job in rep there. I think it would do me good. I wanted to let you know.'

'Are you sure you're fit enough?'

'Quite. Morgue speaking? What does that mean?' The voice was suspicious, unremembered.

'Morgue. It's the . . .'

'I thought you worked at Racing.'

'I do,' Adam said. 'We call it the Morgue as a joke. It's the Morgue of hope. The horses that people bet on never win. All good tips come here before they die.'

'Is that true, Adam?' the voice asked, after a pause.

'Yes. Cross my heart.'

'I met a friend of yours down at Chichester. He came and had a drink. His name was Nobble, I think.'

'Nobble? I've met him.'

'He said you worked at doing obituaries. Is it true?'

'I did,' Adam said, truthfully.

'When you met me, was it because . . .'

'I'd always wanted to meet you.'

'Were you doing obituaries then?'

Adam would not answer.

'Purefoy told you, didn't he?' he said.

'The Raker has never told me anything about you. Perhaps we should not see each other tomorrow.'

'You must see me. Please. I can explain.'

'Yes,' the strange dry voice said. 'That is why we should not meet. I am afraid you can explain.'

A click, a rasping murmur, no more.

Adam replaced his receiver. He stared in front of him at the green files. The letters stretched vertical and horizontal, an alphabet into which the mess of humanity was ordered. From the first bawl through the weaning days to the second time of bare gums, from totter to dodder, from pram to crutch, from hairy to bald, from all fours to upright to stoop, in trivia and toil and tedium, in spurt and lag and waste, each and every span of twenty thousand days and nights reduced to a brown envelope and a paragraph of opinion and a tab on the drawer of a file. Life contained, life remaindered, life in a docket, life in a jacket. Was this the face that launched a thousand ships? Was it? No face, only a line of print, a poet's razor, slicing the skin of beauty's countenance into strips to trace the shape of words. Not lost but gone before. Yes, lost, because gone before. The face unseen is gone, is gone, is gone before. Joyce into Nada is gone before.

The telephone wailed again. In hope, Adam took the receiver from its cradle.

'Joyce? This is Adam.'

The sound in his ear-drum was brisk, sardonic, remembered.

'Noyes speaking. Not your slut.'

'Noyes?'

'The same. And not dead yet. Do you hear that, Quince? I'm alive and kicking.'

'Kicking me, as usual?'

'Right on your lug-hole. I got the X-ray back. My cancer's a sort of wart. Dead as a doornail, and so easy to remove a Boy Scout could do it with that thing for taking stones from horses' hooves.'

'That's good news, Noyes.'

'For *me*, yes.'

There was a pause. Adam contemplated the pyramid of objects on his desk. It rose as high as his thumb. Not much of a relic for three years down in the Morgue. And Noyes was still sitting in judgment upstairs, triumphant, scabrous, petty, in power.

'Why aren't you gone, Quince?'

'I'll be out in five minutes. I've just finished clearing my things.'

'Put 'em back.'

'Why?'

'I can't live without you, Quince. The Morgue wouldn't be the same happy joint with you gone. I need your smiling face to disinter the stiffs. You remember the proverb, You Can't Take It With

You? It's wrong, like all proverbs, which is why so many of our fool readers believe them. I can take you with me, Quince. Beyond the grave. But I can also take you back with me. I was dead, and am alive again.'

'And I was alive,' Adam said, 'and am dead.'

He put down the receiver on to the four arms which bore its weight, like the four black arms of pallbearers. He picked up the paper-clips one by one. One by one he dropped them into an open drawer of his desk. They made small smacks on the guaranteed teak. Adam knew finally that he would stay buried alive until he was retired. The wages of sin were quick death, but the wages of earning a living were slow death.

PART THREE

The Raker

Imagine, there are still some people who maintain that, when the head is cut off, it knows for a second perhaps that it has been cut off – what a thought! And what if it knows for five seconds? . . . Paint the scaffold so that only the last step can be distinctly and clearly seen in the foreground; the condemned man stepping on it; his head, his face is as white as paper, the priest is holding up the cross, the man greedily puts out his blue lips and looks and – *knows everything*. The cross and the head – that is the picture, the priest's face, the faces of the executioner and his two assistants, and a few faces and eyes below – all this can be painted as a background. That's the kind of picture.

from *The Idiot* by DOSTOEVSKY

13

DIDSBURY had shrunk in decades of rain. It fitted Adam's memory as his boy's clothes would have fitted his man's frame. His home street, wide as a river, dangerous as rapids with the passing cars killer as logs, was a mere seven paces across. The doors on to the roadway, once as high as castle gates, would make him duck to enter. The two scrubbed steps up from the pavement had been full battlefields for soldiers. Now they were hardly high enough to trip over. The row of terrace housing was once a Grand Canyon, its tiles scraping the shins of God, its foundations deep down on Satan's shoulders. Now the houses looked what they were, jerry-built Victorian workers' cottages, overdue for demolition. Although Adam had often boasted that he was slum-bred, his actual memory had pictured a mansion on the backdrop of his boyhood. With a start, he realized that he had been telling the truth. His home had been in a slum.

Number 44 was no different from its neighbours. Its door was green and dirty. Lace curtains threw up their iced spray to hide the rooms behind the windows. Above the curtain in the front room, the polished corner of a vast piece of furniture suggested solidity in the interior. The front room had been the only place where Adam had been forbidden and where he had never wanted to enter. He remembered the few occasions when it was used to entertain or marry or bury the family. The heavy furniture and the stale smell of the settee and the chairs had been tear-gas to his youth. Everyone spoke in whispers there, as though they were frightened to disturb the holy silence of the room, and the dust. Although Adam's parents had left the house ten years ago, the front room had obviously not changed its nature. It would remain the front room, shrine-like and unvisited, until the Council bulldozer came along to stove in the house wall.

Children played in the street, and mothers came to doorways to gossip and yell at their offspring. Two old men sat on wooden chairs against walls in places where the sunlight had long ago been known to creep. They did not recognize Adam, coming in his dark and smart overcoat on this pilgrimage to the past. And he did not try to extract recognition by talking with them. He was the one who had got away. He was best forgotten, although he could not wholly forget.

Adam took a slow bus to reach the centre of Manchester. Even the blackened barracks of the old commercial buildings and the palace of the railway station could not repress the sneer in Adam. Once a visit here from Didsbury had compressed in a few miles the voyages of the Argonauts to the end of the world and the Golden Fleece. Now Adam knew London. And Manchester was only what it claimed to be, the second city in the kingdom. More virtuous, perhaps, harder-working, more dedicated to the values of thrift and creed and toil and wages, and to the second-rate.

Yet, even though Adam had crossed the ditch dug between the North and South of England below Nottingham, he could not now despise the capital which had made him the man that he wanted to be. When he had been a child, he had firmly believed that all England below the Trent was soft and sinful, a slattern land where tarts and layabouts would pluck any Northern gull who lighted there, would draw out his guts and pack him home without a patch of down to hide the shame of his bare skin.

Now it was Manchester that was black. And if the grime was the dirt of pride, the arrogant knowledge that Manchester *was* lilywhite within and did not need a wash to advertise its obvious goodness, Adam could only yearn for the white walls and palaces of Westminster. The South had been his bogy and was now his opportunity. The North made him uncomfortable.

The repertory theatre, where Joyce was playing, advertised its opening time at half-past seven o'clock. Adam reached the stage door an hour before the performance. The door-keeper was not in his box of wood and glass. Adam walked down some stone steps and along a corridor of dressing-rooms. A yellow light had difficulty in swabbing back pools of darkness. On each off-white door, there was a card holding a name. One read, NADA TEMPLE-TON. Adam knocked on the door. His knuckles left a white smudge, outlined by a line of dirt on the wood. A voice spoke behind the door, as distant as any voice from a closed room.

'Come in.'

Adam opened the door. Joyce was sitting at her dressing-table, in front of a mirror. She was streaking her face with sticks of make-up. The bulbs on the mirror made the grease-paint shine on her skin like goose fat. She was absorbed in putting a ring of health on her cheeks from a stick of red make-up. She dropped the stick and leaned towards the mirror to begin the process of smearing the colour into a lifelike appearance. She did not turn to look at Adam.

'It's yours truly,' Adam said.

Joyce swung sideways. Her hand fell. The red on her cheek shone wetly as a sore.

'You? I didn't ask you.'

'I happened to be in Manchester,' Adam said, 'visiting my roots. I thought I might drop in.'

Adam could see that Joyce was longing to tell him to go. But her manners triumphed. It is always better to avoid a scene.

'Sit down, Adam, while I make up. I have to go on soon.'

Adam sat on a hard chair some yards away from Joyce. 'I'll see the performance, Joyce. Perhaps we could dine afterwards.'

'Don't stay for the play. It's not worth it. I'm not good enough yet. I've been too long away. I'd rather you didn't stay.'

Adam blessed Joyce silently for the tact of her refusal.

'I could be in Manchester tomorrow,' he suggested.

'I'm afraid I'm visiting friends in Cheshire.'

'Where the cheese and the cat come from.'

'Yes, Adam. Where the cheese and the cat come from.'

Joyce again absorbed herself in the business of putting grease-paint on her face. Her concentration was absolute. Adam was looking at a stranger. Then he realized that all her limbs and her attention were directed towards one action. They were not free to wander where they willed. They were contained within as narrow a cage as the Raker always put upon himself.

'You're taking your acting very seriously,' Adam said.

'I have to,' Joyce said. 'Now I'm on my own.'

Adam felt hope tug within his ribs.

'On your own? What about Purefoy?'

'I said I couldn't see him again, either. He took it very badly. I hope he doesn't do anything silly to himself.'

Joyce began to tone down the highlights on her face with a white stick. She drew broad streaks of white over her temples and cheeks.

'The Raker won't hurt himself,' Adam said. 'He's the world's wonder for self-preservation. But surely you have to see him again? I thought he *made* you.'

Joyce turned her face towards Adam. The white streaks of paint gave the effect of bones breaking out of her skin. Adam felt himself shiver, although the room was warm.

'The Raker did make me once,' Joyce said. 'But now I'll have to start making myself. I shouldn't have stayed with him so long. It wasn't good for my acting.'

'When did you break with him?'

'Down in the country. I got this offer of a job. He told me I should refuse. In effect, he said he'd go on keeping me as long as I liked. I took the job. I just couldn't . . .'

'You've got to keep yourself to keep your self-respect,' Adam said complacently.

'Don't patronize the Raker,' Joyce said sharply. 'He's ten times a better man than you.'

Adam swallowed. 'Why did you leave him for me, then?'

'I didn't know you, did I?' Joyce said. 'Anyway, I refuse to explain. If you couldn't see then, you'll still be blind now.'

'I want to know.'

'You can't ever know. Either you feel it, or you never will. There are no explanations in human affairs, Adam. Only *being* something. There's nothing to *say*.'

'That's a fine way out for you,' Adam said.

'I told you. You won't keep me if I want to go. I do. From you and from the Raker. I have to.'

'Why? My love . . .'

'I'll tell you about *him*.'

Joyce began to smooth the white streaks into the paint below. Her hands worked over her face. Its pale shine waxed more and more in the glare of the bulbs. She seemed to have grown plump in the cheek, almost an Alice to Adam's eyes.

'I did drive once more, Adam. We were driving Nobble home. I said I'd take the wheel. Nobble was in the front seat beside me.

The Raker was in the back. I began to step up the speed. Nothing much. Sixty perhaps. But we hit a sharp corner. We drifted a bit. As the wheels locked, I had a look in the mirror. And there was Death looking back at me. I tell you, Adam, it was Death.'

Joyce turned towards Adam. Her hands stopped rubbing in the grease-paint. They began to dart forwards and backwards, emphasizing the story. They had broken out of the cage of her will. They were on their own.

'There was an eye. Cut in half by the mirror. Another eye, to the side, below. A bit of a mouth, thin, at a slant. Two holes, nostrils, or gaps. Yet all was white. Like glare. White to make you blind. White as fire. White as salt in sun. White. The face of death.'

Joyce could not speak for the memory. Adam waited. She stayed silent. Adam was impatient.

'It was a hallucination?'

'Worse. It was the Raker. He'd been thrown forwards in the seat. I'd just caught his eyes and face in the rear mirror. But I pulled up sharp. I let Nobble drive. And I told the Raker I couldn't see him again.'

'Did you tell him why?'

'Yes. I could have forgiven him even then. It was a trick of light, his face like death. Foreshortening. A funny angle. It wasn't his fault if I saw him look like Death. But he answered,' her voice imitated the Raker's precise diction, '"*I* look like Death? My dear, what a compliment! I have been striving for that effect all my life."'

Adam laughed. He thought that Joyce had intended a joke. He wanted to seem on her side, with humanity against mortality.

'He does look like death warmed up,' Adam said. 'He's not like you and I. Breathing.'

Joyce turned back to the mirror.

'Not you and I,' she said. 'I'm on my own. I told you.'

'Why?'

'You repeat yourself, Adam.'

'Why?'

Joyce took up a small stick of blue grease-paint to outline her eyelids.

'Because,' she said, 'you are like the Raker. You are slow death to me.'

'I'm not,' Adam complained.

'You worked at death. Even mine.'

'I had no option.'

'Then you're a coward. There's always a way out.'

'It was just temporary.'

Joyce turned finally on Adam. Everything in her face and body seemed to tremble, except for the curious stillness of her neck which kept her head erect and square on her shoulders. She was once again the creature of contrary movements that Adam had known. Each part of her was on the point of springing into life. Her voice raced and stopped and raced again.

'All of us. All of us, just temporary. I want to forget it. Do you remember, in the hospital, I said I didn't have a past? I was a phoenix, three days old? I've had a third birth. Since I saw Death in that mirror again. Third time, he'll be lucky. He'll get me. I've no past now. Can't you see? I don't want a past. Not you. Not the Raker. Just life. Now. No one who knows me. No one who thinks I broke my neck. People to come. Be. Go. As they are *now*.' She paused, then suddenly screamed, 'For God's sake, go away.'

At her scream, Adam rose. He tried for a last time to master the situation. She was hysterical. She needed a firm hand.

'When you've calmed down . . .'

'Go away.'

'The North,' Adam appealed desperately. 'We could see it together. We're both Northerners. Damn the bloody South.'

'Go away.'

Adam backed towards the door. He opened his mouth once more, but Joyce screamed again, 'Go away.'

As the door closed until Adam could only read the card, NADA TEMPLETON, he kept a last image of Joyce. She was springing to her feet, her arms waving, her legs trembling, her body in a shake, her hair tossing, in a frenzy, a mania, a riot of being, breaking free.

14

LOTTIE was old.

Adam had never noticed anyone cross the borderline between middle and old age. In his world, the categories were fixed. No one was elderly until they had retired from work. And when they had retired from work, they had the decency to retire from circulation. Old age was unheard because it was unseen, except in the cases of pensioners in pubs or flower-sellers, who seemed natural in their advanced years. Their youth was out of mind.

When Adam had lived with Lottie, he had considered her mature. Maturity was a good word. It suggested ripeness, apples sweetening in attics, wisdom, brandy, knowledge of the world, and fat life-policies. Her struggle against her thickening flesh had been almost saintly in its dedication. She had mortified herself with mechanical belts, with the fists of masseurs, with steam, with mud, and with injected paraffin wax. She had martyred herself in order to preserve herself. She was her own good cause.

But Adam had been away for several months. Although he had prepared the possibility of his return, he had not prepared himself for the new situation of Lottie's age. He had carefully planned his surprise entrance. He had called after breakfast, and had hushed the maid with the bribe of a pound note. He had wished to creep on Lottie unawares, so that she would wake to his face. He could pretend to her that she had fallen asleep for months, from the day that he had left her to work out his struggle of conscience. But now that his divorce was on the verge of being declared final, he had come back to her. He was the prodigal son, perhaps, but he did not expect to encounter a fatted cow.

Yet, as he had inched open the bedroom door, he had seen a heavy figure squatting on the bed, turned away from him. The back was bowed, but the head was upright. Below the white plastic hood that hid the hair of the creature, a roll of flesh swelled on the neck. The pink and flowered wrapper was stretched tight across the shoulders and ribs. Bulges and crevices beneath the material

suggested more flesh pouching on the bones. The lines of the back
from armpit to buttock were convex. The creature had no waist.
And the bed itself was depressed under the weight of the sitter.

As Adam crept forwards, the figure did not budge. Adam could
not believe that it was Lottie. But as he moved to the side of the
shape, so that he could see the drooping tent of the front of the
dressing-gown and the puff of skin under the jaw, he recognized
his past mistress. There was a straggle of red hair from the hood
and a length of sharp nose that reminded him. And, as he remembered, Lottie turned her face upon him.

Cleansing cream had wiped away her mask. A slight oil was a
varnish on every down-dropping line, every crack, every fold of
skin, every dewlap. The past months seemed to have brought defeat
to the expression, or perhaps mere resignation. The features were
not prepared to struggle any longer. The brave face to the world
had been put aside, leaving only a look that anticipated the draw-
ing-out of the days. Adam realized that Lottie must have lied to
him about her age. She was well into her fifties.

A harsh voice spoke, its grit not yet creamed by morning coffee.
'How did you get in?'

'A surprise,' Adam managed to say. 'I wanted to give you a surprise.'

'Get out,' Lottie said. 'You can wait till I'm ready.'

'I'm late for work already.'

'Then get out altogether.'

'I'll wait,' Adam said. It was not that he wanted to wait, since he
could see that he would never come back to Lottie. But he could
not leave in this manner. He had been told to go the day before,
and had gone. This time he would be kind. He would stay to show
Lottie that he was not repelled by her.

Lottie took only a quarter of an hour to appear in the sitting-
room. She had done little to herself. She had removed her plastic
hood; but her red hair was pulled back tightly from her forehead, as
though she were wearing a skull cap of a different colour. Her face
was hardly made up, except for a touch of rouge on lip and cheek,
and a little eye-shadow round her lids. Her brows were growing
in their natural place. She had changed into Chinese slippers and
a mandarin house-coat, stiff with velvet and braid to conceal the

shape of the body. Only her trick of throwing up her chin to catch the light reminded Adam that she had once used all the armoury of perpetual youth.

'I hope you're sorry,' Lottie said.

'I am,' Adam said. 'I assure you, I meant it to be a happy surprise.'

'Calling at this ungodly hour after not giving a sign of life for months? I might have had somebody else in bed with me.' Lottie's boast was mere vanity. She said it, and she did not mean it.

'It would have served me right,' Adam said.

'It would. Why are you here? Did she kick you out?'

Lottie seemed to have acquired the brutality of the old, whose years grace their tactlessness by the name of eccentricity.

'She?'

'That actress. Enough people were glad to tell me. Templeton, isn't it?'

'I was just helping her through her convalescence. She broke her neck.'

'Now she's got too well for you?' Lottie walked across the room to ring the bell for the maid. As she did so, she caught sight of herself in the huge mirror over the chimney-piece. She immediately threw back her shoulders, then winced at some twinge of rheumatism, and stooped again. 'I've let myself go a bit since you left.' She rang the bell. 'Suddenly it doesn't seem worth it any more.' She swung on Adam. 'You don't look too young yourself these days.' Adam moved a pace sideways. He looked at his own reflection. He noticed no change in his curls or his smooth cheeks. Perhaps the mouth dropped open a little more fatly. He pressed his lips together.

'I'm just the same,' he said.

'Absence makes the sight grow sharper,' Lottie snapped. The maid came in. 'Coffee and toast for two, Ann.' The maid nodded, and left the room. 'You'll stay for breakfast, of course.'

Adam did not like Lottie's air of certainty. The invitation was a command. 'No,' he said. 'I must rush.'

'The dead can't sleep quietly without you,' Lottie said. 'I'd quite forgotten.'

Adam was piqued.

'Was I so very easy to forget?'

'You?'

All at once, the fat old woman by the mirror stopped listening. She withdrew inside herself. For a strange moment, Adam felt like an eavesdropper. He need not have been in the room.

'I've been thinking a lot of Ralph,' Lottie said. 'Just sitting and thinking. When he was alive, we used to travel everywhere. I never got much outside the hotel rooms. I can't stand the heat, you know. I wish I had. All I can remember is those damn hotel rooms. The punkahs and the air conditioners always made a racket. Either you suffocated or you didn't sleep. I don't sleep much now. It's not because of air conditioners . . .'

The old woman's voice trailed away. She was lost in the windings of her mind. She went to sit on the sofa with the white seat. She lolled back comfortably. Her breasts were bags of meal under her house-coat.

'You begin remembering. It doesn't stop. You eat and you remember. And the days and the nights are much the same. No one calls. And if they do, you're out.'

Adam took his cue for a going away with dignity.

'I'm sorry I disturbed you,' he said. 'I'll go at once.'

The old woman ignored him.

'You know the most important thing for a woman? It's not marriage. Not her first child. Not when her husband dies. It's the day she decides not to wear a corset any more. You don't know the relief. To get up one morning, and never wear a corset again.'

'I must be going,' Adam said. 'I'm sorry to have disturbed you. I really am.'

Adam began to walk away. He expected Lottie to call after him, to beg him to stay, to clutch at her last lover, to weep, to play the ageing woman with her final finger-tips on the young. But all he heard was an indifferent voice, saying, 'Please don't bang the door.'

*   *   *

Adam took the day off to move his effects from the house where Joyce lived to another service flatlet. His new room was dreary in the way that the clean and functional depresses. Every object and corner had an edge like an axe. Adam could hardly walk across the room for fear of slicing his shins off on a square chair-leg or a square table-leg or a square bed-leg. Even the basin, the only rounded shape in the room, was tucked away in a cupboard.

The colour scheme was equally modern, a gradation of tasteful pastels in search of a primary colour. There was nothing to irritate or engage the eye in the whole room. Sight could not dwell here. It could only skid off the antiseptic surfaces in search of some scrunch of waste paper to contemplate.

Even when Adam had set out all his objects, he found the room intolerably regular. His clothes were packed away into drawers, his papers into the desk. Two hairbrushes and a comb on the shelf by the square mirror, and the print of a Modigliani nude on the wall, were hardly enough decoration to persuade Adam that he was cosy. The accumulated data of his life was still stored at Purley. He missed the cricket photographs, the clutter of old rackets and fishing tackle, the Landseer print of a stag at bay. Joyce had given him the taste for litter as the sign of home.

Adam had carried a legal letter in his pocket all day. He had not dared to slit it open. Now he despised his cowardice. He thrust his thumb roughly under the flap of the envelope, and ripped it open. The letter told him that the Divorce Court had judged him in his absence on an undefended suit. Alice had been granted a divorce on the grounds of his adultery. She was given custody of the child. Her marriage with Adam had officially ended. He was liable for the costs of the case.

Now that the break was complete, Adam felt ready to forgive Alice. She had driven him away through her melancholy and un-willingness to keep pace with his career. But now that he had freed himself from the ungrateful Joyce and the aged Lottie, he was pre-pared to go back to his wife. For the sake of his son, he would put up with Alice and save her from the trough of her desperation all her remaining days, till death did them part. She needed him, and Adam would satisfy that need. These were the true costs of the case.

The nobility of his future was a plaster on Adam's bleeding pride. He had been wounded, and now was healed. He would re-turn, strong enough to do his duty. He would complain no longer. He would merely accept his responsibilities. He would endure the

Morgue and his wife to feel himself the good man he basically was. If a job's worth doing, his father had often said, it's worth doing well. Adam suspected that his job was not worth doing. But now, in the name of duty and family, he would do it even better.

Adam caught the train to Purley, prepared to make his old life new.

15

ADAM stole a piece of binding twine from the station platform. He had a use for it. When he reached the front door of his old house, he set to work to repair the broken trellis. It was an easy job. In three minutes, the trellis no longer sagged. It stood upright with its neat wooden diamonds as a windy wall to the porch. Adam pressed the door-bell, one resolution to the good.

Alice answered the door. But it was a changed Alice. She had lost more weight. She was only a little heavier than she had been at the time of her marriage. Her hair was, indeed, permed into a neat mess of matronly curls. But she was wearing a pink shirt and a pair of cherry-red trousers that almost gave her the youthful look of a drum majorette.

'Adam,' she said, as though she had need to identify him. Then she swung round in a complete circle in her red trousers. 'Look. I haven't been able to get them on for five years.'

'You look splendid,' Adam said.

'I feel it.'

Alice led the way into the hall. Tin trunks gaped open their maws on the carpet. Piles of clothing made monumental staircases for mice. China objects, wrapped inside old paper, were mines to the feet.

'I'm sorry for the mess,' Alice said. 'I want to get ready well in time.'

Adam could not understand. Alice could not move without him. She was surely helpless.

'Where are you going?'

'Australia.'

If Alice had said Nova Zembla, Adam could not have been more surprised.

'Australia? What for?'

'I want Peter to have every opportunity. It's a new country. It'll be waiting for him when he grows up.'

'But how'll you *live* there?'

'I'll find a job,' Alice said with confidence. She posed, a hand on each hip, her elbows protruding. 'They're short of secretaries over there.' She smiled, as if the uncertain prospect pleased her. 'It'll be a challenge, won't it? A new life, really.'

Adam could not think of what to say. His entrances all seemed to have gone wrong. While he changed, other people changed. It was unfair that they did not remain static until he returned to them. Adam felt flayed in the sudden idea that his friends and his women had lives of their own out of his presence.

'I mended the trellis,' he said lamely.

'Good. You'll put up the house for sale, I expect. It's all yours. Unless you want to come back and live here.'

'There won't be much left over from the mortgage. What are you taking?'

'All my clothes and Peter's. A few ornaments and kitchen things. Nothing else. We want a clean start.'

Adam probed for the weakness in Alice. There must be something behind her confidence. She could not have escaped the dependence of their years together so quickly.

'But you haven't got any money.'

'God will provide, the Vicar says.'

'And you believe him?' Adam laughed. 'You'd do better to elope with the Vicar. Then God might provide.'

'He's too good a man,' Alice said simply. 'And I don't need to depend entirely on God.'

'What a terrible admission!'

'I would, if I had to. God has provided me with the strength to go. But Aunt Gladys provided the money.'

'You never had an Aunt Gladys.'

'I had forgotten her, I admit,' Alice said. 'She's not really an aunt. A sort of half-great-aunt. But she did keep track of me enough to tell her lawyer. I got the letter with a cheque a week ago. Two thousand and a few hundred she left me. There's a little more to come. God rest her soul.'

Adam was silent. It was monstrous. The living could be forgotten. And yet, when they died, they did not forget the family that lived after them. The money of the dead could free the living. It could free them from dependence on those who did not forget them. The legacy of a stranger had cut the last tie Adam had with Alice, her need of his financial support. There must be laughter beyond the grave.

'If you need any more help, Alice . . .'

'I've got quite enough, thank you,' Alice said. 'There's a Court Order that you have to help with Peter, anyway.'

'I don't like your going off just like this.'

It was Alice's turn to laugh.

'We're divorced, remember. You don't have a word to say about what I do or don't do.'

'Are you sure it's right for Peter? He mightn't like Australia.'

'It's a perfect country for small boys. He's cricket mad, as you know. He can't wait to get there.'

'I'll miss not being able to see him,' Adam said. 'Can't you think of me?'

Alice looked seriously at Adam. Her eyes were round in her face, as solemn again as they always were in the stare of his memory.

'I've been thinking of you too much,' she said. 'All these past years. I couldn't think of much else. Why you left me, who you were with, what you were doing, would you come back? Now I'm going to Australia. And I don't think of you any more. It's wonderful. Not to think of you any more. I'm thinking of myself. And Peter. With God's help.'

Outside, in the garden, Adam heard Peter shout. He could not answer Alice for the bitterness in his mouth. He was only relieved that she had stopped him from making a fool of himself by asking to crawl back to her. He walked past Alice into the sitting-room and out through the french windows on to the lawn. Peter was whirling round and round, his hands clutching the loop of a rope tied to the apple tree. When he had whirled himself into dizziness, he let go and tried to walk down the lawn. Shrieking, he fell over and lay laughing on the grass. The rope was a noose above him.

Adam walked over to his son and stood above him. His heart twitched to see the small creature on the grass.

'Hello, son,' he said. 'Hello, my son.'

Peter squinted upwards through the decreasing circles of whirligig sight.

'Oh, it's you.'

He began to rise. Adam bent and gripped him by the waist. He pulled the small boy off the ground, holding him dangling a yard in the air.

'Your daddy's still got some muscles,' he said.

Peter's face reddened. He struggled. 'Put me down,' he screamed. 'Put me down.'

Adam set him down. Peter immediately recoiled a pace.

'You hurt me,' he whined.

'A man doesn't mind being hurt a little,' Adam said, 'if it's all in good fun.'

Peter recoiled another pace. His face was ludicrously solemn, as though Alice's melancholy had become his inheritance.

'Why are you here, *Father*?'

'I came to visit you, Peter. And your mother.'

The boy scowled.

'You're divorced. You went away from us. For ever. Mummy says it's like being dead.'

Adam looked at the defiance on the child's face. He saw the tears beginning to form at the corners of the boy's eyes. He did not know what to say, now that Alice had begun to turn his son's mind away.

'Don't you still love your daddy?' Adam said.

'No,' Peter said.

He ran, head down, towards the french windows. Adam could see him sobbing as he ran. The boy reached the windows and disappeared into the house. Adam walked slowly after him. While he was still outside the house, Alice came to the french windows. She held both sides of the frame of the windows, barring his entrance.

'You'd better go,' she said coldly. 'Round by the side. You've upset Peter.'

'You've been poisoning his mind against me.'

'I've told him the truth,' Alice said. 'I thought it was best that way. He wanted you to come to Australia with us. He couldn't understand.'

'You've done a wicked thing,' Adam said. 'You've made him hate me. His father. Is that Christian?'

'God's truth is sometimes a terrible thing, the Vicar says. It can set sons against fathers. Or wives against husbands.'

Adam felt the anguish of total isolation burst like a belch within his ribs.

'Forgive,' he cried. 'Can't you forgive?'

'Goodbye, Adam,' Alice said. She held out her hand. 'I do forgive you, of course. But Peter and I want to be left alone now. That's all.' Adam took her hand and tried to squeeze it, but she withdrew her arm behind her back. 'You might look in at the shed as you're going round. I've put all your junk there. I'll leave the house clean and tidy when we go so you can sell it at once. I wouldn't like you to think I didn't know how to treat you decently, even though we're divorced. Goodbye.'

Alice closed the french windows. Adam heard the key turn in the lock and the bolt slide home. The last vision Adam had of Alice through the glass was her pink back and red legs walking out of the room. By the door, Adam could have sworn that Alice gave a small skip like a child for joy. Or she may have been tripping over the leg of the coffee table.

Under the cobwebs and warped roof of the shed, Adam's treasures were stacked. Certain articles were visible in the heap. The old schoolboy's cap with the yellow tassel. The fire-screen, embroidered by his grandmother. Rackets and golf clubs and rods and football boots and a hockey stick. A copper ash-tray won in a golf medal competition. A china duck for shooting straight in a fairground. A tufted assegai from South Africa. And an ancient horse-pistol with a barrel as wide as a drainpipe.

Adam stooped and picked up the pistol. For a moment, he played with the idea of putting its muzzle against the side of his head and pulling the trigger. Of course, it was not loaded; but the action would show the sincerity of the intention. He would go through the motions of suicide. But there was a sudden scurry and whimper and movement in the barrel of the pistol. He dropped the weapon in fright. A small brown shrew ran out of the muzzle and scuttled away down a hole in the corner of the shed. Adam would have laughed, if his heart had not stopped briefly from the shock of the shrew. The pistol had been loaded with a bullet of ravening life.

16

BRING out your dead.

The cry and the crier. Where? Nowhere. In the mind only. Bring out your dead. The cry of the death cart. Bring out your dead. The plague dead. The Great Plague dead. Bring them to the living Adam.

Cars are death carts now. Cars with two yellow ovens, in the night burning, in the night coming. A horn is blowing. And so ordered, that the sweepings and filth of houses be daily carried away by the Rakers. They shall warn of their coming, by the horn blowing.

Brandy is history in the head. Data of the pulped daily column. Brandy near Marble Arch, brandy after brandy. Reeling down the night street to the bus stop. Hold the slippery pole to keep upright. What if you've fallen? All men are fallen. This bus goes down Tyburn Way. Tyburn Way. Where the execution carts started. Off with the sentenced, off with their heads. O the crowds pelting filth and jeering! It's a long long way to Tyburn, it's a long long way to go. We'll never get there. We hope we'll never get there. But if we do, they'll hang, draw and quarter us. With the mob howling. While we hear them, we're living. Howl for us living. Howl.

Look, the executioner. Black mask, silver axe-blade. Noose round our neck, choking. Rip out our heart now. Show it smoking to our eyes. Life after death for seconds. Long enough to see our own heart smoking. Then chop us into quarters, take them down to Wapping. Hang them in chains there, till the three times tides' grace, saltly purifying. Stick our heads on spikes in Whitehall. Like the great Cromwell. Three years buried, then dug up. Head on a spike for twenty more, till a wind blew it down to a sentry. See the great Cromwell with the wart on his nose, only two-and-sixpence. Cromwell is a mummy, dead two times over, dead and alive again, dead and gone.

Again the horns blowing. Raker, where are you? The Raker is coming. He is on the double-decker, off to the City. That's the way to Tyburn, to final execution. Whet your axe for me, executioner. I'll give you a shilling. Make it clean, Jack Ketch. One stroke, and I'll pay you. I'm on my own now. No one to live for. All gone, all gone. All lost and gone before. Look at me, ye lost ones. High-riding on the double-decker. Going to Tyburn, high on the bright plague cart.

'One to Tyburn, conductor.'

'Is shilling, to the City. No go Tyburn.'

Give him his shilling. Is he my executioner? Jamaican in a blue uniform. Chop me with your machete. Down Oxford Street, we go gawping. Oxford Street, huckster alley. Selling since Judas first was selling. Woods, beads and honey. Swords, furs and bees-wax. The caravans strike out to Middlesex. The deep forests of Middlesex. Out drive the City traders. Ruffs, jewels and farthingales. Artisans to Soho. Muffins and comforters. Come buy, ye people. Come buy. Stalls rise six storeys. Stockings, woollen to silk to nylon. Codpieces and corsets, crumpets and cameras, ambergris and cotton goods, what you need we'll sell you. If we don't have it, you don't need it. Welcome to the world over. Spill past our windows. Choose now and pay for it. Cash on the nail, please. Saunter and deliver. Spend a pound for a purse to put your pound in. What you name, we'll make it. All except money. That's for your making over to us.

Down past Kingsway, sweeping under the offices, out into Holborn. Who is this fusilier, standing with his bayonet, fifteen foot in the air, high as the high-rider on his bright plague cart? 22,000 fell in the Great War? O Royal Fusiliers of the City of London. They shall not pass. But the plague carts pass in their brightness, past your bronze bayonet, past the Tudor timbers of Barnard's Inn, on down High Holborn, with the buildings rising. St. Paul's through the spaces, high-hat over the buildings. Dome of a Wren, big skull for a little brain. How great the human head, if such its past doing?

The City is deserted, vacant and empty. No business at the Bank, then, Bank of All England? Stock-jobbers and brokers, buyers on discount, mercers and grocers, gone, gone to the suburbs. Rush Hour, Rush Hour? The hours all rush, rush away, gone, gone. Once men and women lived in the City. Above the counting-houses, children instead of guineas. Ale and coffee, gambling and spitting, cock-fights and harlots, oranges and lemons. That was a City that was a city. Now it is no city. For it is night-empty. A bare gut at midnight. No one to hear me. Bring out your dead, to my bright plague cart.

Time to descend now. Down the iron stairway. All the way to hell now. 'Mind the step, suh.' Down the hell of the side streets. Cobble on the alley. Down towards the river. Tower and river. London river and Tower of London. Dock, wharf and crane, and thew of London. City built on water, on the fruits of water. But when London's burning, London's burning. Pour on water, pour on water. Not all the water of the Thames can end the burning. Burn down the City, Great Fire from Pudding Lane. Burn down the City, to end the Great Plague there.

Down along to the Tower. Traitor's Gate dropping. Bloody Mary, Bloody Mary, with big-blown belly, swelling in false pregnancy. Bloody Mary, puffing the flames for the heretics. Bloody Mary, dead in the chapel. Bring the faggots, light the fires, burn them, burn them. Burn the plague out of London. Plague of heresy. Plague of treason. Plague of anarchy. Plague of reason. Plague of foreigners. Plague of Papists. A Plague on all your houses. London's for the burning.

Up Tower Hill, across to the railings round Trinity Square Garden. Seek peace, seek peace. Peace where the ships get orders. Neptune points down-river from Trinity House portico, points out their course to the far-sailing mariners. Points the way to sure wreckage, the last salt sinking. On the temple of the garden, another inscription. No temple of Love, of Wisdom, of Hunting. A temple to the drowned dead, the deep drowned.

1914–1918
TO THE GLORY OF GOD
AND TO THE HONOUR OF
TWELVE THOUSAND
OF THE MERCHANT NAVY
AND FISHING FLEETS
WHO HAVE NO GRAVE BUT THE SEA

Over the five-foot spikes. Pain in a foot pressing. Leap down,

stagger into the garden. Faint light in the black night. Bronze dol-
phin rising, by white steps falling. Black plaques with black letters
in memoriam. Lean by the first plaque. Strain eye. Repeat the letters, of Masters mastered, Jack Tars weighted, full fathom sunken,
bell bottom deep.

A.D.C. 527
OF UNITED KINGDOM
ROSS J.B. *Master*
FOSSETT E. J.
PARRY, O.

Abbas Combe
BRISTOL
EDWARDS T.
FITZPATRICK C.
JOHNS F.
OLIVER G. H.

Abbey Dale
LONDON
BRUCE N. D.

Abbotsford
GRANGEMOUTH
WATSON A. J. *Master*
BLACK W.
FOWELL R. C. . . .

God, are there Morgues everywhere? In every garden? In every
garden a Gethsemane? Names in their catalogues. Dead men living
dead. Shall we remember them? We shall remember them. We
cannot forget them. For remembrance cannot perish, as we perish.
It lives on in names, names for the living. Move along the black
plaques. A yellow flower in a pot below a black panel. Flower for
whom, giver? What ship did he sail on? *Ardanbam,* Glasgow? or
Ardenvohr, London? or *Ardeola,* Liverpool? or *Arica,* London? or
Arinia, London? or *Ariosto,* Hull? or *Arletta,* London?

So ends the panel. Which ship held your sailor? Which dark hulk rusting? Or does it matter, sailor drowned dead, bell bottom deep?

Reel to the green horseshoe. There's a marble wheel, grass-set. A wheel with sixteen fingers. Compass pointing with sixteen fingers. North, Nor' Nor' West, Nor' West . . . Sixteen ways to wreckage. Where shall I escape? For the world is round as the compass is round. Fleeing, in my hull driven, somewhere, the sixteenth finger-nail of God will scrape my ribs, stave them, and down, down, down, down, down to hell I go.

A horn blows on the river. Fog coming from the Dogger. The Raker? Coming in fog from the Dogger?

Up the steps again, turn right. In the dark, red geraniums round a square, six foot by six foot, cobbles round two more inscriptions. Read them, read them, in the faint night lights. Eyes are for the recorded endings of the world without end for suffering, for suffering of men, amen.

> This Site Has Been The Scene Of
> 75 Executions: The First Was
> That Of Sir Simon Burley In 1388
> And The Last That Of
> Simon Fraser, Lord Lovat, in 1747

Simon to Simon, head after head rolling. This is the end of Tyburn Way. Here on the bright plague cart riding, or from the Tower falling. Two are specially noted, brave old Jacobites, titled and remembered.

> Site Of Ancient Scaffold
> Here The
> Earl of Kilmarnock
> And
> Lord Balmerino
> Suffered
> 18 August 1746

Who did you die for? Young and Old Pretender? Or was it life the Pretender, and death the only Stuart?

Lie on the cobbles. Put your head on the stone block, support-ing the spiked chains by the geraniums. Loosen your tie. Open your collar. Strike, God, strike. On the neck of this sinner. Sever his jugular. He is the lone one. Unwanted, rejected, by all his kind derided. Adam in his garden. His garden of sorrows. Strike, Jack Ketch Jehovah. Adam, worse than a Jacobite. He hath no cause but himself. And who is he? A recorder of the dead. The Morgue keeper. And he did not see them, for he knew not their souls. The dead all around him. The dead of London.

The horns blowing. Fog on the river. The Raker is coming. The Gabriel Raker. Blowing his horn. On this Night of Judgment.

The graves are opening. Opening the plague pits. Giving up their long-dead. Giving up the rotted, the sore, the wasted. All the rooms of the city are cemeteries. Giving up their long-dead. The badger is walking, down the Fleet river. The dead press about him. Rise, Adam, rise now. Till London is a street map, a forest, an estuary. In the black gaps of streets or sewers or rivers or ditches, the dead pack and scrape each other. And who, who the dead of London?

All from the stews and sweat-shops. All from the parks and bear-pits. All the masters and the lackeys. All the mistresses and tweenies. All the coneys and the ponces. All the mobs from the Garden and Trafalgar Square. All the foreigners laid out as strang-ers. All the tailors and the joiners. All the moil of men and toil of women. All the bawl of children and babies. All the multitude of dogs mute in burial. All crush into the ditches, all, all, dead. So great the clutter the houses bulge inwards, then bulge outwards, from the long-dead pressing within them. The houses split open. In each room, a seething. Tudor rooms and Georgian, chock-a-block with dead ones. Who first sat on your Chippendale, dined on your pewter, rolled in your four-poster? All the past Londoners, long dead, long dead, dead with Queen Anne, long dead and buried and remembered. Remembered by the things they left behind them, their leavings, their sweepings.

O Raker, record them by their sweepings from their houses. Record them for the living. O dead men, infinite in your swarming, countless and soulless. How shall I judge between you, I who must judge between you? There are no rich among you. No poor among you. No age nor sex nor beauty. Nothing of foul, unequal living. Everywhere, a mob of skulls seething. Dried peas in a barrel. Ants on a dunghill. Sands on a dune. Specks on a great wind. Man, all and nothing. Man, plagued dead and burned dead and forgotten dead. And always remembered, by his sweepings.

★　★　★

The horn blows, and blows. The fog comes down. Adam rises wearily. He is their judge. He is their recorder. Until he joins them.

★　★　★

Bring out your dead. For I am one of them.

17

'I'M going to kill myself. Tonight. This very night.'

The Raker sat opposite Adam in his attitude of sympathetic interest. He wore black silk pyjamas and a black silk dressing-gown. He claimed that Adam had not disturbed him from his sleep. He said that he had been sitting awake in an armchair, contemplating the white logic of horror for nearly a week. Or it may have been an hour. He had lost track of time. Certainly, he had answered the knocker quickly when Adam had battered the door with its iron cross. He could hardly have had the time to brush his white hair to its peak of intended casualness. Even the legs of his pyjamas had kept their crease, as though he had not lain down in them.

'What method will you use?' the Raker inquired with kindness. 'Gas has a horrible smell. Heights leave an unpleasant mess. Bullets are unreliable. Ropes are certainly bad for the throat and the composure of the face. The Romans, of course, severed their veins in hot baths. But think of having to endure the sight of that clotting water. Zola did invent the perfect method, I agree. You close the windows of your room and fill all the space with flowers and go to sleep, while they breathe in all the available oxygen. Unfortunately, all realist writers are vague over medicine. It does not work. I have tried it many times myself. Life is unbearable, Mr Quince. But suicide is more so.'

'I mean it, damn you,' Adam raged. He had sought the Raker across London for confirmation and approval, and he received mockery. He was cold and exhausted and reeling. The brandy was now iron in his head. He sat badly in his own chilly flesh.

The Raker smiled. It was his old infuriating smile. He looked the same. Alone, he had not changed in the past months. And yet . . . The bones under his eyes were surely more prominent, his cheeks more hollow, his skin more waxen with the gloss of lack of sleep. His voice was even more precise than usual, as if he were fighting to deny the incoherence and despair of long wakefulness. If Adam had not been lost in his own misery, he might have believed that his rival had insomnia.

'Naturally, my dear Quince,' the Raker said. 'Every sensible man means to commit suicide every morning. Otherwise he could not possibly stagger through until the end of the day.'

'I'll kill myself here.'

'Please do.' The Raker was unruffled. 'What may I offer you? A cheese knife?'

'I'll do it with my bare hands.'

'They say,' the Raker smiled, 'that prisoners have been known to swallow their own tongues. A physical feat, I fear, beyond my own capacities. But if you would be prepared to accept my poor help.' He waved his hand towards a shelf, holding up four china chemists' jars. They were each a foot high and lettered in Gothic script ARSENIC, POTASSIUM, CYANIDE, and HEMLOCK. On each of their china lids, a small cherub sat, pinkly rounded. They were the sort of jars that Adam had seen in stockbrokers' houses as a joke, containing candied fruits.

'I'll die laughing,' Adam said. 'You poseur. I don't know why the hell I came here.'

'Surely you wished to kill yourself, as I do, daily.'

'Then why don't you? Do you funk it?'

The Raker sighed.

'You could call it that. Unfortunately, my cowardice is also my philosophy. As my life has made little or no difference to my species, neither will my death. So life and death are much the same thing to me. I find I cannot choose between them, especially as I avoid all choice. Then there is the simple biological fact that it is pleasant to feel alive. When our blood is warm in our body, and our hands do what we tell them, it seems a pity to destroy such intricacy. I must confess, I am too comfortable in my own skin.' The Raker paused. 'There is another point. Do you remember, in Schopenhauer . . .'

'I never had enough time to waste reading philosophy. I had to earn my living.'

The Raker ignored Adam.

'Schopenhauer says that suicide is really the expression of the will to live. When you kill yourself, you kill yourself *for* something

or someone. Although my own will to live is so feeble that I have
never supported any cause or anyone, I fear that my suicide might
persuade the world that I cared enough to die for it. A fatal miscon-
ception! Schopenhauer thought one should negate the will to live
as far as possible. And then, contemplate. Although what exactly
one contemplates when one does not want to live, I cannot imagine. But at least, by avoiding any action either good or evil, one has
a clear vision.'

'Words,' Adam said. 'Words. Words. They don't *mean* a damn
thing to you. You live on your bloody words because you don't
want to do anything.'

The Raker lifted a hand and rubbed his cheek-bone. The lower
lid was briefly pulled down from one eye. For a moment, he appeared to have a deformity, a grotesque squint. Adam was shocked,
yet curiously happy to see the stillness of the Raker at last disturbed.

'Correct, Mr Quince. Always correct. I have never wished to do
anything.'

The Raker rose to his feet and began pacing up and down from
chimney-piece to far wall. He turned round continually in front of
two pictures hanging on the grey and black chequered wall-paper.
The pictures were made of cloth. Both represented stages, with
red curtains framing a green baize background. In one, an old man
leaned on a stick and on the shoulder of a skeleton, who was lead-
ing him into the wings. In the second, a young man playing a cloth
horn danced, while the skeleton tapped, unnoticed, at his back. As
the Raker reached them in his pacing, his head was flanked neatly
by the two scenes of age and youth and death.

'I have never wished to do anything,' the Raker continued. 'One
in three of my species is dying of starvation. Every human being
that I know is suffering, for he or she is a human being. A walk in
the street deafens me with the infinite din of woe. I withdraw to
isolation, as I have during this past week, but I am a coward. So I
am driven out again into company, and I am again distressed by
my own kind. I try to influence no one so as to hurt no one. But
I influence willy-nilly by my very breathing. Each time we move,
Mr Quince, the heavens change. So I try to influence deliberately
by influencing little. And yet even my inaction is a sort of choice. I

choose not to do, and by not doing, I choose to tolerate the errors that others commit. Because I fail to protest, I am applauding the miseries inflicted on mankind by men. Do unto others, Mr Quince, what ye would they did unto you. I do little unto others, thus I would what is done unto them by others. I sit and wait, because I cannot stand the screaming of my race as it lives. But as I laugh louder, the cries grow louder. Lately, through these walls, I have been hearing the groans of our damned species. I cannot avoid them. Finally, I know. I cannot avoid my kind.'

The Raker's voice was serious. His walk had become agitated. Even his hands shook a little. Adam had come in the middle of the night in search of sympathy. Now he found himself expected to sympathize. He was angry that he could never play any of his chosen roles.

'Damn humanity,' he cried. 'We can't do anything about the starving millions. It's just luxury to pity them. Self-indulgence. If you can't help them, it's phoney to make yourself feel good by weeping for them. Better forget them. I've got a worse bug, Raker. Joyce. She's left me.' Adam could not resist adding, 'And you, I gather.'

The Raker continued his pacing.

'Yes. One is alone, Mr Quince. No more blindness that isolation is escapable. We sit with our selfish selves. We wait for some parasite to come and destroy us. We fill our time with collecting stupid objects, trying and failing to sleep, consulting doctors who can merely tell us that we must die sooner or later.'

'We're working too.'

'We are working too, in order to forget that we can change little or nothing. The world is a vast concentration camp, Mr Quince, handed on to future generations. All we can do is run it well or badly, and I do not know which is the greater sin.' The Raker paused, then added, 'Have you ever studied the ant?'

'Never.'

'Come. Let me show you.'

The Raker ceased his pacing to pick up a flat oblong box, covered by green cloth. He brought over the box towards Adam and set it on the table in front of him. He drew back the green cloth. Adam was looking through a pane of glass into a series of passages between earth or sand. The passages weaved in and out of one another as intricately as veins. For an instant, Adam was reminded of his vision of the City, as he looked down from the sky.

'This was once an ant colony. There are seven survivors. My only other friend, an over-optimistic naturalist called Hellys, presented the colony to me last week. He could not bear keeping it any longer. He told me its history. If I may, I will repeat it, the story of how it diminished to its seven survivors.'

By looking closely at the passages, Adam could see first one, then three, then seven ants crawling along their ways. They were pale in colour, as though their original blackness had been rubbed off on the floor of the box.

'The ants you see are miserable things, hatched from eggs after the death of their queen. Hellys bought the colony when it was thriving. The queen was healthy, the workers ran about doing their duty, the winged ants were fed and prepared for their one mating flight. Then Hellys went on holiday, and forgot to feed the colony for a few weeks. During this time, the queen died. The colony was now doomed, and it began to behave like all doomed colonies of men. You must realize, of course, that ants are even older than human beings. Our species has perhaps existed for thirteen million years – the ant, twenty million.'

Four of the surviving ants carried round with them small white specks. The other three combined to carry an object resembling a minute hook. Adam did not know what they were doing.

'On the queen's death, the ants split into two parties. A tug of war began round the body of the queen. It broke in half. Each party of ants then paraded their section of the body of the queen around the colony in triumph. They washed the queen's severed body, cleaned it, tried to feed it. But the queen was dead and divided among herself. The last batch of her eggs was looked after and hatched. You see the seven ants from this final brood. All the rest of the colony has died. The body of the queen has been mauled so much by its many processions that only its abdomen is still in existence. You can see the remnants of the womb of the queen still being carried about as a talisman. The other objects they carry are sterile eggs. But the seven must soon die. For the queen is dead, and the eggs are barren.'

Adam pulled the green cloth over the ant colony.

'Take it away,' he said. 'I don't like your friend's sense of humour. Though he couldn't have chosen anyone better to give it to. Anyway, we've got nothing in common with ants.'

'I wish we did,' the Raker said, picking up the box and replacing it in its old position. 'We would not be happier, but much better organized.'

Adam felt outmanoeuvred. He was about to die. And he could not get his audience to applaud his resolution.

'I am going to die,' Adam said. 'This night. You will live.'

The Raker stopped his pacing. He put his hand on the lid of one of the china jars. He looked at Adam. The smile returned to his mouth.

'Are you sure that I cannot offer you a little hemlock, Mr Quince? It is my favourite. I have always thought that Socrates had the best of taste.'

'You can give me a brandy and soda,' Adam said sulkily. 'Why don't you take the *hemlock* yourself?'

'Why not, indeed,' the Raker said. 'I can think of no reason.'

He went over to a cupboard in the corner of the room, and opened its doors. He took out two tumblers, a bottle of brandy, and a soda siphon. He poured brandy into one glass, and squirted soda into both. He took the tumblers across to the china jar marked HEMLOCK. He set the glasses down on the shelf. He grasped the china cherub, pinkly rounded, and removed the lid off the jar. His hand shook a little in the sudden weakness of fatigue. The china rang against the wall.

'Are you sure you will not join me in a little hemlock?'

'What the hell is in there, really?'

'Hemlock.' The Raker smiled. 'What else?'

Adam's eyes travelled slowly round the room, from the chimney-piece with its five *memento moris*, past the pictures on the wall in praise of death or still-lives, past the grey silk hangings, past the copies of Egyptian and Etruscan mummies to where the Raker stood by his mock poisons, with his hand plunged within the jar.

'Everything's fake here,' Adam said. 'And you're the biggest fake of all.'

The Raker took his hand out of the jar. His palm held some

dark grains. He seemed to be holding a palmful of brown sugar.

'You are sure that you will not join me in a hemlock?'

'Brown sugar in brandy,' Adam said. 'You're crazy.' He rose and walked over to the Raker and took his brandy and soda off the shelf.

The Raker dropped the brown grains into his glass of soda water and stirred them with his forefinger. Adam could not understand the vulgarity of his action. The Raker no longer seemed to care about the effect that he was making.

'Don't tell me you're going to drink that muck.'

The brown grains dissolved in the soda. The Raker carefully replaced the lid on the jar marked HEMLOCK. He did not lick his wet finger. He picked up the tumbler, which now contained a dark liquid, almost purple.

'That's like brown sugar,' Adam said. 'It must be Barbados. Don't drink it, you fool, just to impress me. It'll make you sick.'

The Raker looked at the tumbler for a moment. There was uncertainty in his expression, that look of slight distaste which made Adam hate him as an aristocrat. Then he shut his eyes, lifted the glass, and drank down the dark liquid in three gulps.

His mouth puckered until it was no bigger than a thumb. He lowered the tumbler. A bland look returned to his face, the smoothness that had been missing since Adam came into the room. He began to smile and opened his eyes.

'Very easy, really.' His smile grew broader. 'I could never have imagined it was so easy. I pretend to believe literature. Why should I be so surprised, then, when it turns out to be true?'

'You'll be sick,' Adam warned. 'Barbados sugar and soda. Revolting.'

'I had better walk it off, then,' the Raker said. 'I believe that is the remedy recommended in the *Phaedo*.' He began pacing up and down the room.

'What's that?'

'One of the rather boring pieces of philosophy I glance through to pass my apathy. It does not advocate suicide, incidentally. It says that a man ought not to kill himself before God makes it necessary for him to do so. But since Rimbaud said correctly that Dieu Est Mort, we have had to be our own Gods. So I suppose we have to judge the time of our necessity ourselves. Although every minute, if rightly judged, makes dying necessary.'

'I've judged my time,' Adam boasted. 'My time is up tonight.'

The Raker smiled again. He was pacing with determination now, as if he were a sentry guarding the sleep of royalty.

'I always admire men of action,' he said. 'Especially when they provoke a reaction in the inert like myself. Without you, my dear Quince, as my example and witness, I would still be sitting in my chair, waiting in horror for the sleep that never comes.'

'Don't you care I'm killing myself?' Adam said.

'What can I say? I can congratulate you on your good fortune. I can hope to see you in some future life, in which I disbelieve. Or – ' here the Raker's smile grew so broad that it might have been called a grin, if the term had not been ungentlemanly – 'I can follow in your footsteps.'

'Don't you mind about Joyce leaving you? Of course, you never cared for her as I did.'

The Raker stopped pacing, then seemed to reconsider, and began to pace again.

'As you know, it is a subject which I will not discuss. Nada, in my opinion, was right to leave both of us. When we first met, I think I said that one of us would have to die . . .'

'It's me all right,' Adam said.

'One of us would have to die. In fact, it would be best for her if both of us did. We are, as the phrase goes, the kiss of death.'

'Don't lump me in with yourself. That's how you drove her from me.'

The Raker's pacing pounded the floor. One board had begun to creak each time that he passed above it. He seemed determined to walk himself into the ground.

'We have only ourselves to blame, if we have no one to blame for being human. You are like me, Adam Quince. Or if you are not, you will become like me.'

'Never.'

'When you first arrived, you told me of your vision of the dead in the City.'

'It was the brandy in my head.'

'It was the truth. I have seen worse every night for twenty years.

And once you have seen it, you are always aware. Did you read the *Journal of the Plague Year*? The book that I recommended?'

'No,' Adam said. 'But I did skip through it.'

'Better to have run through it, or never to have seen it at all.' The Raker's paces were a bell to his speech. 'In it, Defoe tells of a piper, who did badly during the plague, and used to say that the death cart had not come for him yet, but they had promised to call for him next week. One night, he fell down drunk in the City, as you did. The plague cart came along and carried him off. It stopped on the edge of a mass grave. He woke there, and rose, and said, "But I ain't dead though, am I?" Then he returned to his piping and drinking. Defoe does not say what his experience did to the piper. But in Vienna, a street singer, Max Augustin, was actually thrown alive and drunk into the plague pit. He struggled up from among the dead and wrote a song.'

Here the Raker began to sing in a pleasing voice, curiously bass in note for so thin a man. All the time, his paces were an accompaniment to his song.

> 'Each day a feast we had
> The plague is now so bad
> Corpses only to be had
> O how sad!

> 'O Augustin, my dear
> Lie down upon thy bier
> Alas! Vienna dear
> All gone, I fear.'

The Raker's pace continued to beat time after he had ended his song.

'All gone I fear, Adam Quince. Once into the plague cart or pit, there are no more feasts. Only a waiting for the next cart. All gone.'

The Raker had begun to pace more slowly. He seemed, on the sudden, to have difficulty in lifting his feet. Adam despised him. The other tired so easily. But what could you expect from a man who lived so soft a life? His insomnia could not be that bad if he could knock himself out with such facility.

'It's not only Joyce,' Adam said. 'My wife's going to Australia. I could do without her, although she'll never be able to do without me. She'll be back in a few months, her tail between her legs. But my son Peter. He's a funny little nipper. I'll miss him. Australia will be too tough for him.'

The Raker walked over to a drawer of his desk. He opened it and took out a brown envelope. It was similar to the envelopes that Adam used for working in the Morgue. He also picked up a postcard from the drawer. Very slowly, he walked back to the sofa and sat down. He lay back against the arm of the sofa. He then used both arms to lift up each leg on to the seat of the sofa.

'Excuse me,' he said. 'I am a little fatigued. After so much sleeplessness, one becomes suddenly weary.' He took a fountain-pen from the table beside him, and began writing slowly on the envelope and the postcard. 'I hope you will forgive me. I must catch up with the last of my correspondence. It seems to have been piling up all my life.'

'Christ.' Adam jumped to his feet. 'My death's at least an important matter to *me*. I'll go.'

The Raker turned his head as though he could no longer bear its weight.

'It is to me, my dear Quince,' he said in a tone of great kindness. 'I promise you. Your death matters to me. Please stay.'

Adam was mollified, and sat down again. Ever since his last drink of brandy, a curious sense of well-being had stolen over him. He was warm again. His muscles had relaxed in his chair. He felt pleasantly sleepy. So he yawned in enjoyment, with the silent laugh of a man happy at the prospect of imminent rest.

'Excuse my lack of manners,' the Raker said. 'For once, manners seem hardly important. Strange, when my whole life has been bound up with them. Confess, Mr Quince. Your chief reason for hating me has been my manners.'

'They're so bloody superior,' Adam said. 'I'm just as good as you.'

'Far better.'

'Better if you say so. I always think you're looking down on me.'

'Looking up to you,' the Raker said. 'Admiring your grasp of essentials. You never go beyond what you must have. And, indeed, there is no reason to do so.' The Raker paused. 'Would you switch on the fire, my dear fellow? If you would.'

Adam leaned forward and switched on the electric fire in the grate. He thought that the request was strange. The atmosphere in the room was already close.

'Yes, I admire you, Adam. May I?'

'Of course.' Adam almost liked the Raker for this odd touch of fellowship.

'You are so courageous. You choose to live in this world. To be part of it. To suffer all it makes its sharers suffer. You submit to all the sins, the original sins invented by our time, Adam. But I? I withdraw from the world. I live in another century. I suffer no modern sins nor virtues. For I shun the day. I do only the duties which I set upon myself. I live well within my means. I wait to die. Adam?'

'Yes.'

'I have mentioned you in my will. Of course, for such a coward as me, one who takes such exquisite care of himself, it may be many years . . .'

'It's no use to me,' Adam said coldly. 'I said I was killing myself tonight.'

'But suppose. Suppose Nada were waiting for you outside. Suppose you had a change of heart. A new soul. A will to live without suicide.'

'I don't change my mind about important things,' Adam said. 'I've specially chosen a room with gas.' For a moment, he could not remember whether his new room had gas or not. Naturally, it would have. All service flatlets had gas-meters.

The Raker wrote slowly on his postcard. It was only a short message.

'My legacy, probably futile, will be the objects in my house. The rest will go to Nada. I thought perhaps you might find room for them.'

'You could bury them in my coffin,' Adam said. 'Judging from all this junk, a coffin would be a damn suitable place to store it in.'

The Raker smiled.

'I have no choice, do I? When I first heard of your profession, I knew that I had found my heir. Ridiculous, this urge to pass one's own errors on, but only too human. You are a recorder and judge as I am, Adam. You should always be looking at the beginning and the end.'

The Raker finished his writing. He placed the brown envelope on the table beside him. He left the postcard on his lap.

'I can't make you out,' Adam said. 'I always used to think you were a fraud and a phoney. But you're so damned *consistent* about it.'

'I fear I do repeat myself, Adam.' The Raker was speaking very slowly now. He seemed drugged with weariness. His head lay back heavily on the arm of the sofa. 'I chose a deliberate part to play. Not believing in the soul, I have had to learn enough simple actions to persuade people that I am not a monster. And I have played my part. At least, verbally. Now you come and point out rightly, by your example, that words demand deeds. If I despair . . .'

'You should logically kill yourself,' Adam said. 'Like me. But you never will.' Again Adam could not repress a yawn. The muscles of his neck and shoulders stretched and relaxed deliciously beneath his skin.

'Not for the moment,' the Raker said. 'Adam, perhaps I could help you a little about your death. Do you know what Socrates talked about when he was going to die?'

'No. I don't.'

'Firstly, he said that dying was easy. He was right. He said that philosophers found it especially easy because they studied all their lives how to die. He was again right. If you live each day as if it were your last, Death is hardly unexpected when he calls.'

'It's all just a pose,' Adam said. 'Familiarity breeds contempt.'

The Raker lay very still. His lean shoulders and profile on the arm of the sofa reminded Adam of a past scene. Of Joyce, when he had first seen her, lying on the board in the hospital, the weight on the wire at the back of her broken neck.

'No,' the Raker said. 'Familiarity breeds con*tent*. You accept what you know well. Know Death each day. Be glad to see him.' The Raker was silent, then he continued. 'Socrates also told his friends that dying was necessary for living. The one produced the other. As life must end in death, so death must end in life. It is true, although not in the way that Socrates said. He thought the soul might live after death. I know our body is merely a part of the great chain of the living and the dead. One umbilical cord back to the first mother. One cord to hang us all. We are bound, Adam, in death and life. We cannot, cannot forget this.'

As Adam looked at the pale face of the Raker, he began to love him. The Raker seemed lost in his own vision as Adam had been lost an hour before in his vision. He was treating death seriously, and Adam had come to him for the first time to hear of death treated seriously. For Adam feared his own near death.

'I like you, Raker,' Adam said. 'I like you, man.'

'Thank you, Adam.' There was no gratitude in the Raker's low voice, almost a coldness. 'Look, I am weary. Would you forgive me? I know you have business to do. Your own death. I know it is urgent for you. Could you come here, please.'

Adam rose and went across to the Raker, where he lay, smiling a little, unmoving, on his sofa.

'This postcard,' the Raker said. 'Would you be so kind as to post it?'

Adam bent to pick up the postcard from the Raker's lap. As he did so, he lost his balance. He put down a hand to steady himself. He gave a hard push in the Raker's lower ribs. 'I'm sorry,' Adam said. He righted himself, the postcard in his hand. 'I hope I didn't hurt you.'

The Raker was still smiling.

'I did not feel a thing,' he said. Adam wondered at his extraordinary self-control. He admired a man who did not wince when he was pushed in the ribs.

'Wish me luck,' Adam said, drawing the edge of the postcard like a knife across his throat. He knew it was the sort of remark that the Raker would like. As he brought his hand down from his throat, the postcard itself caught his eye. It showed a drawing of Pierrot and Columbine drinking at a ball. They were framed by curtains in a bowl of light. As the eye looked more closely, the bowl of light became the brow of a skull. The heads of Pierrot and Columbine were the sockets of its eyes. Pierrot's hanging sleeves were holes for nostrils. Their drink glasses were teeth. The table-cloth was the jaw-bone. Love in death.

'Your postcard is very apt,' Adam said. 'You should have sent it to me.'

The Raker nodded.

'I wish you luck,' he said. 'Goodbye, Adam.' He did not move from his position. Adam walked towards the door. He stopped before going out.

'I'll see you in hell soon,' he said. 'Literally.'

It was then that the Raker made a remark so vulgar and inconsequent that Adam could not believe his ears. He would have been less shocked if the Raker had belched. The last words of the Raker that Adam heard were, 'Adam, we owe a cock to ass . . .'

Adam stood where he was.

'What was that?'

The Raker did not reply. He seemed to have dropped off to sleep. His long insomnia, followed by his pacing, had lulled him. Adam closed the door softly on him, and left the house. He felt strong and warm. His feet were springs beneath him. He even skipped once, like a child, on his way to the letter-box, where he posted the card. Then he set off more slowly towards his own room. He had remembered that he was to kill himself.

18

Why not?

The two words written on the back of the postcard, addressed to the Morgue, burned in Adam's brain. *Why not?* All Adam's hatred of the Raker flared within him. The precious bastard. Adam made an oath to keep alive until he was ninety years old, just to spite the Raker. Why should his rival have the right to sneer in advance at him? And the final insult was that he had posted the Raker's card to himself the previous night. The Raker had disbelieved him in his midnight agony. That false show of fellowship at the end of their meeting was a sham to lull him into posting his own sentence of humiliation. The Raker should sweat in hell.

Adam turned over the postcard to look again at the Pierrot and Columbine in their skull of light. He began to tear up the card into small strips. These strips he ripped into squares. When he had reduced the card to a heap of paper fragments, he swept the remnants off his desk into the waste basket. But he was not rid of his anger so easily.

He had meant to kill himself until his walk home. But the night had been cool and quiet. The streets had been washed with a light rain, so that the pavements in the lamplight were as beautiful as the wet skins of seals. Peace had settled upon Adam. Although the corridor to his new flatlet had smelt of stale tobacco and inevitable cabbage for all its modern and boxed finish, he had found his own room welcome. Its bareness had reminded him of a monk's cell, a place where he was always talking of retiring. In his reaction from the idea of death, he had reacted from the studied clutter of the Raker's objects. Life had seemed to him again worth while, if it were kept trim and useful. He had located the gas-meter and had found, to his annoyance, that he did have a shilling in his pocket for buying gas. But he had told himself that a shilling's worth of gas might not be enough to kill him. Suicide was not something to botch. A job worth doing was worth doing well. So he had left the shilling in his pocket and had gone to bed. He had sent himself to sleep with the reassurance that he could always kill himself in the morning, if he still felt like doing so. In the morning, he had gone to work in the Morgue.

Why not?

Adam looked up at the green filing-cabinets all about him. The letters on their white cards were black teeth in square mouths. The letters grinned like the false teeth grinned in the skull on the postcard. The handles on the cabinets were curved upwards, as polished and fixed as the Raker's sneer. God rot him!

Adam picked up the telephone and dialled the Raker's number. He would tell the Raker where he could go for ever.

'Hello. May you rot.'

'Who's that?' a careful voice said in the receiver. It was not the voice of the Raker.

'Adam Quince speaking. I want Purefoy. It's important.'

'Adam Quince?'

'Yes. Could you get Purefoy for me?'

'Could you tell me where you are speaking from?'

'What's that to you?'

'Mr Purefoy has been taken seriously ill. We are looking after him. If you could come round as soon as possible. We need to make certain inquiries.'

'Are you the police?' Adam asked.

'Friends of Mr Purefoy. Could you come round please, Mr Quince? You will not be difficult to trace. At once, if you please.'

Adam put down the receiver. It was certainly the police. The Raker seriously ill? It couldn't be the Barbados and soda. Or had there been something else in the jar marked HEMLOCK? The Raker had certainly been unnaturally tired the previous night. But poison acted quickly. And there was no reason why *he* should kill himself.

Adam left a note for Noyes, saying that a friend was ill. He gave the Raker's telephone number. He caught a taxi in Fleet Street. On the way to Belgravia, he saw sickness everywhere. The sky itself was in a fever of yellow near the horizon, a sulphurous flush beneath black clouds. The passers-by stooped at the shoulder, or bent over canes, or shuffled along the pavements. Where there were young girls walking briskly, they had too much redness in cheek and leg, as though their blood was about to burst through their skins. The taxi-driver himself had a bandage round his neck over a boil. The Plague was imminent on London.

A police inspector did open the door to Adam's knock. His face was white beneath his blue-black cap and white above his blue-black collar. He had been taught the trick of looking suspects firmly in the eye. In another profession, his stare would have been called rudeness.

'Mr Quince?'

'Yes,' Adam said.

'Come in.'

The inspector waited for Adam to enter and followed him down the hall to prevent his escape.

Adam had viewed the scene in the sitting-room many times. A photographer was fixing the scene in black and white. Policemen and a doctor were examining the body on the sofa and the objects in the room. The place no longer had the look of a museum, but of a buzz of lively business. The fuss of official activity over his body did not seem to disturb the Raker himself. His face was as waxen as usual. He lay in perfect composure in his black dressing-gown and pyjamas. His hair was brushed into its casual place. Only a faint blueness round his closed mouth and closed eyelids suggested that he was dead.

'There's an envelope for you here,' the inspector said. 'It contains various clippings about Mr Purefoy. Can you give us any idea about his death?'

'When did he die?'

'Late last night.'

'You said he was seriously ill.'

'You might not have come, if you had known the truth,' the inspector said.

Adam turned to the police doctor, a small, bald, cheerful man.

'What did he die of?'

'Of hemlock poisoning,' the police doctor said. 'Very rare. Very rare these days.'

Adam's throat contracted. There was bitterness in his mouth.

'How does hemlock work?'

'There's a very good description of its action in Plato's dialogue, the *Phaedo*,' the doctor said. 'Socrates was forced to drink hemlock, after being sentenced to death. To make it work quickly, according to Plato, you walk about until your feet grow cold. Then you lie down. Gradually, the poison spreads upwards through your legs and stomach. You feel colder all the while. When the hemlock reaches your heart, you die.'

'Can you talk all this time?' Adam asked.

'Yes. Socrates was talking to his friends until the last moment. Do you know what his dying words were?'

'We owe a cock to ass?' Adam said.

'You make it sound a bit crude if you don't complete it. What Socrates actually said was, "Crito, we owe a cock to Asclepius; pay it, and don't you forget it."'

'And who was Asclepius?' Adam said.

'Can't you help us?' the inspector said, staring at Adam.

'This is important to me,' Adam answered.

'Asclepius? My own professional God,' the doctor said. 'The Greek God of Healing. I suppose Socrates said that, because death by hemlock is such a civilized way of dying. Rather like a slow pain-killing drug you don't ever wake from. Asclepius himself was the greatest of all doctors. He's meant to have raised people from the dead.' The doctor turned back to his examination of the Raker's body. 'Not your friend, I fear.'

Adam stood still. He had watched the Raker die, and had not understood. If the Raker's death were true, he might always have spoken the truth. He might have *known*, after all.

'Now will you talk?' the inspector said, with impatience. 'Why should this man have four jars, all filled with poison, clearly marked on their labels?'

And Adam told him the story of how he had watched the Raker die.

19

Adam sat at the Raker's kitchen table, reading the contents of the brown envelope, which were clipped together in order. On the envelope, the Raker had written:

For Adam Quince
Ash From Spent Days

On the top of the clippings, there was a short letter. It had been written several months previously. The Raker had been preparing for his death for a long time, for perhaps all of his life.

My dear Adam,

I hope you will excuse my impertinence in entrusting these last relics to your expert care. Since our recent first meeting, I feel that only you can do justice to my existence. My life has been trivial, and I feel sure that you will succeed in expressing its quality perfectly to the few who may wish to hear of my end. I have done little that is worth recording and nothing that is worth preserving.

I was born obsolete. My name is genuine Norman, and my family have always been successful robber barons. A thousand recorded years have conspired to produce me. And yet, I cannot remember a time when I did not feel out of date. I would rather let the sad story stop with me than struggle to adapt myself to a new time. Yes, Adam, you may well found a line of wealthy bandits; but I am happy to end mine as soon as possible. I am out of my age, and I wish to bury the past with myself. There is no use for me. As the price of keeping power in the present was the making of sausage skins, you will understand my decision to prepare for the reasonable death of the Purefoys.

But I have one trust to leave to you.

This afternoon you asked me why I was called the Raker. I

told you that Rakers were appointed during the Great Plague, and it was so ordered that the sweepings and filth of houses be daily carried away by them, and that they give notice of their coming by the blowing of a horn.

You already possess to perfection the techniques of our trade. You have learned to reduce the sweepings and filth of all our lives and houses to a few sweet words. You are the Raker now, not I. Do with my filth what you must.

JOHN PUREFOY, *Gentleman*

Adam looked at the blank surface of the table in front of him. It was no more helpful than the blank surface of his desk at the Morgue. He was in the familiar situation of his trade. He had to judge a man's life by his few leavings. Or sweepings or filth. Only this victim claimed to be his future self. He began reading the evidence for his verdict on the life of the Raker.

The first item was a birth certificate. It stated that forty-seven years ago, a certain John Purefoy had been born to Michael Homer Purefoy and Emmeline Purefoy, née MacAlister, in Oxford, England.

The next item was a letter, dated six years later, from an address in Surrey.

Dear John,

Your mother and father are gone away for a long time. I am afraid that you will not be seeing them again. Your Aunt Mary and I will keep you in our care. I have been appointed your guardian and trustee, something which I will explain to you when you are older. Try to think of me as a father and your Aunt Mary as a mother.

Your pocket money will be raised to 1s. per week.

Your loving uncle,

ADRIAN PUREFOY

Next came a school report on John Purefoy, aged eight years, Form V, St Leonard's Preparatory School for the Sons of Gentlemen, Godalming, Surrey.

John is a happy child, who seems to gain a great deal of

benefit from the games and outdoor activities of the school. His low place in form is due to his long periods spent in the sick-room, suffering from minor ailments. I am sure that his character and health will develop rapidly in the coming years, when he has learned the satisfaction of 'mens sana in corpore sano'.

RICHARD ST EVANS, *Headmaster*

Next came a poem from the St Leonard's School Magazine, written by John Purefoy, aged ten.

I am the little king
Sitting on my throne
And although everything is mine
I am the little king alone

I am the little king
But when I go to bed
I have no biscuits in my tin
I do not have some bread

I am the little king
All say that I am, I am
But if I say, Do something
It seems that no one can

I don't want to be the king
No, not for anything
I want to be a little mouse
Inside my little house

Then there was a letter in a schoolboy's scrawl. It had no date.

Dear Jonny,

I'm sorry you were straped again. Don't blub. I have been straped ten times, and I dont blub now. I want to be your friend. Ill swap my 4 hundreder conker and my knife for your three spirals,

DICK

The schoolboy's letter was followed by another letter from Adrian Purefoy.

Dear John,

Enclosed is a certificate, which you may exchange with my stockbroker, for five pounds' worth of Consols for your fifteenth birthday. They will be worth more each year. Thus I would advise keeping them all your life.

Your Aunt Mary and I will unfortunately be away in April. I have, therefore, made arrangements for you to stay at your school over the holidays. Your Housemaster's report says that your work leaves much to be desired, while you have failed to distinguish yourself on the sports field. I hope that you will profit by this occasion to catch up on your studies and to practise your games. You should be grateful for the splendid opportunity you have been given to complete a first-class education. You will be proud of the 'old school' for the rest of your life.

Your Aunt Mary sends her love and I add my regards.

ADRIAN PUREFOY

The next clipping was cut from an undergraduate newspaper at Cambridge.

At the Union last night, John 'Raker' Purefoy (Trinity) opposed the motion 'That the English upper classes are bloody and should be bowed.' In an effete defence of privilege, he maintained that anyone who endured the private hell of a public school deserved all the pleasures that later money could buy. 'I am rich,' he declared, 'and am therefore different from most of you. I may add, I intend to stay that way.' He was shouted down by an angry House. The motion was later carried by 323 votes to 31, all, it is reported, from the Boat Club.

Next, there was a letter in an old-fashioned copperplate hand. The paper was thick and expensive, something of the texture of vellum. The Raker had written in the margin, *Died 1950, A friend.*

My dear John,

Thank you for your gift of a dozen bottles of port. I should not accept it; but I assure you that every glass will make my sin more bearable. I have enjoyed having you as my pupil. You have a casual, arrogant, brilliant mind, which is always a delight to tease and to stimulate. I could only wish you one stroke of good fortune, that you lose all your money. I cannot expect you to give away your inheritance. I personally would not. I am only glad that I never inherited anything. That is the richest inheritance of all, the bequest of freedom.

I noticed in a recent speech of yours in the Union that you paraphrased Scott Fitzgerald's remark, The Rich Are Different From You and Me. You are rich, and you are different from the rest of us, although your originality has nothing to do with your wealth. Of course, life will be easy for you materially; but I do not envy you your choices. Your duty to your family will lead you to continue the business of making sausage-skins. Your duty to the privilege of being born rich will force on you the need to dedicate yourself to the service of others, in order to satisfy your own conscience. You may choose to ignore your duties and retire from the world, as I have done in this College. But I assure you, it is impossible to retire from the world. People will draw you out, as contact with you has drawn me. We meet each other, we influence each other, we cannot forget each other. I shall not forget you.

Yours sincerely,

DENNIS ALWYN

Again, there was a letter from Adrian Purefoy.

Dear John,

Although I have no further legal powers over your estate, now that you have reached the age of twenty-one, I feel it incumbent upon me to say that your intended action is wicked and irresponsible. Your father and your grandfather worked all their lives to build up the name of Purefoy into a name with a world-wide reputation for excellence and quality. In my presence, you have often made slighting remarks about sausage-skins. But can you be so heedless as to ignore the wishes of tens of millions of eaters of sausages spread across the world, who rely on the name of Purefoy on their product? British Made still means best.

The financial irresponsibility of your action is a betrayal of the trust that your father put in you. But it is not, as you well know, grave for yourself, as you will have an income of several thousands of pounds a year from other sources. It is the principle of your action that is evil. You intend to make over control of Purefoy's Skin Company to its employees and working men. Such an action strikes at the foundations of our society, which is based on the principle of responsible control. I quite understand that your action is, as you state, not one of Christian charity, for you are no Christian. Nor is it a Communist action, by your own avowal. I am at least thankful that you seem to have avoided the contagion of that pestilential doctrine that is sweeping the universities in these sad times of ours. You state that you are making over the family business to its employees, because 'you don't know how to run it, and you don't care who runs it, you don't even eat sausages, and good luck to those who are fool enough to make them, let alone pig enough to eat them.' I would advise you, if you persist in this schoolboy irresponsibility, to make over the business to your relations. We certainly possess the feelings of self-sacrifice and dedication needed to run this great concern in the spirit of its founders.

I warn you, if you go through with this childish folly, you need expect no more help and affection from your Aunt Mary, who is heart-broken over your action, or from me. We have cared for you since your parents' unhappy accident, and we are now reaping the fruits of your selfish ingratitude. If your dear father, my brother, were alive, I am certain that he would make it impossible for you to do the crime which you intend to commit.

Look into your heart, and consider one last time whether you wish to preside at the liquidation of the Purefoy trust, honour and duty.

ADRIAN PUREFOY

This letter was followed by a clipping from a national newspaper.

MILLION SAUSAGE FRY

A fire gutted the premises of Purefoy's Co-operative Sausage-Skin Factory in North London last night. The efforts of twenty fire-engines were unavailing. No cause has been ascertained for the blaze. Union officials deny that recent labour troubles in the 'co-operative' firm have anything to do with the fire.

Playboy ex-Sausage King, John Purefoy, who made over the factory to his employees on his coming of age, took the news without concern. 'Nero fiddled while Rome burned,' he said to our own reporter. 'I idle.'

The following report was stamped WAR OFFICE ATTENTION and was headed *Secret and Confidential*. It had a note pencilled in the margin in the Raker's handwriting, which read, *Stolen by me from the Commanding Officer's tray in order to prevent my transfer to Mandalay, or some other jungle spa.*

PUREFOY, JOHN, *Capt.*   12.10.1942

He carries out his duties in the Battalion strictly in accordance with Standing Orders, and thus he cannot be officially faulted. On the other hand, he will never do anything under his own initiative. Nor does he seem to care about the British winning the war. Although he has never expressed any Fascist or Communist sympathies, he is not a supporter of democracy, or of anything. He has a disastrous effect on general morale. He has stated that the human race is doomed and that he wishes to accelerate the process. Once he persuaded several young officers to play Russian roulette with an old pistol. One of them was taken to hospital, with nervous prostration. When I reprimanded him for this action, he demonstrated that the single bullet in the pistol was, in fact, a dud. He said that he was proving that courage depended upon an illusion.

He delights in mocking his superior officers in such a way that no official charge can be brought against him. He is highly intelligent, but he takes pride in misusing his intelligence to disrupt the great efficiency of the Battalion under my command. I recommend his immediate transfer to the Far East, where he can only do mischief to himself, or to the enemy.

FARQUHAR FRASER, *Lt.-Col. Commanding*

The following item was a medical discharge from the army on the grounds of shell-shock and acute nervous depression.

Two postcards, dated 1946 and 1949 respectively, were the sequel of the medical discharge. The first showed the beach at Nice, and the second showed the Lido at Venice. Both held messages scribbled in the same rounded female writing.

The first ran:

Dearest John,

I don't believe you. I know I can make you happy my darling. Only try, try to love me half as much as I love you. This dreadful war is over. We will find peace and joy together. Please don't write things like 'While there's death there's hope' to me again. I know you don't believe it. You are just hurting yourself and me.

Always your loving ANNIE

The second ran:

Dear John,

Richard and I are staying with his parents, Sir Arnold and Lady Cynthia, at the Lido. I am happy to tell you that he has agreed to my asking you to be godfather to our little Adrian. I am sure that you will remember him generously throughout your life; he is named after Richard's cousin Adrian, your kind uncle. Christening in May.

Yours

ANNE (Golightly)

From 1950 to 1960, the Raker had merely left certain gas and electricity bills for varying amounts to commemorate the important events in his life during the decade.

Two envelopes came after the bills. Adam felt a pang, when he recognized Joyce's handwriting. The envelopes were dated at an interval of two years. On the first, a small box gave the name of the sender as *Joyce Howell*; the address began, *J. Purefoy, Esq.* On the second, the box gave the name of *Nada Templeton*; the address began, *John Purefoy.* For a moment, Adam did not dare to examine the slit envelopes further. Then his curiosity got the better of his jealousy. He looked inside both envelopes. They were empty. The written name *Nada* mocked him. And he could almost sense the Raker's smile behind his back.

There was nothing else that the Raker had thought it necessary to preserve.

20

THERE was a knocking at the kitchen door. The police inspector entered.

'Telephone,' he said. 'Someone from the newspapers. You work there yourself, don't you?'

'Yes,' Adam Quince said. 'If it can be called work.'

'What do you do?'

'What you do,' Adam said. 'I collect information about the dead, so that I can lie about them in public.'

The police inspector stared at Adam. His eyes were washed and small.

'Are you insulting an officer of the law?'

'Which law?' Adam said. 'The law that the strong can always oppress the weak.'

He walked over to the door. He felt himself stand tall. Behind him, was the faint single chime of a church clock, striking the quarter-hour. It sounded, for a moment, like the echo of a horn.

'I'm sure your friend's death will make a very good *story*,' the inspector said with contempt.

Adam went over to the telephone in the hall. Facing him, there was a small automat in a glass case. Inside the case, a paper girl in a hooped skirt sat on a paper swing, hanging from the paper branch of a paper tree. Adam twisted the catch on the side of the case of the automat. The swing began to move backwards and forwards as regularly as the pendulum of time. A hidden music machine began to play an unknown tune. Its rills and tinkles were as richly plaintive as the sound of a shaken chandelier.

Adam picked up the receiver of the telephone from the hall table, and put it to his ear.

'Hello. Quince speaking.'

'You take your time,' Noyes said, 'as long as it's time off your job.'

'I fear I am doing my job,' Adam said. 'My friend is dead. Suicide.'

'Who is he? Does he rate a paragraph?'

'Purefoy. John Purefoy.'

Adam heard the sound of Noyes's dry laughter.

'Purefoy. Wasn't he the Sausage Baron? I knew him at Cambridge. Rich as bloody Croesus, and so stuck-up you could sharpen a knife on his nose. What was his nickname? Mucker, or something.'

'The Raker.'

'That's it. The Raker. I'll find a space for him for old time's sake. I'll give him a box. Three column inches deep. Get the obit to me in an hour. A suicide's always worth the space, anyway.'

'There's nothing on him in the files.'

'That's your funeral, Quince.'

'Please find someone else,' Adam said. 'I knew him too well. Or too badly.'

Adam heard Noyes's laughter again.

'You *have* gone soft, Quince. Dirt soft. You know what a friend is? Someone you can rely on – to sell in time of need. But I'll spare your tender parts, God knows why. I'll send a cub round to get the story. Hang on to the body till he shows up.'

'The Raker will stay here,' Adam said.

He put down the receiver, and went to the kitchen to wait.

★   ★   ★

When the cub reporter arrived, Adam led his pudgy willingness into the sitting-room. The police had removed the body and the jars of poison and the tumblers and all smooth surfaces that might hold a finger-print. The disorder in the room and its unaccustomed vacant spaces were strange to Adam. But even more strange was the small depression on the seat of the sofa, where the Raker had lain.

'Where's the corpse?' the cub asked in disappointment.

'The plague cart called,' Adam said, 'and took him away.'

The cub went over to the sofa and sat down cheerfully, plump in the middle. He took out his notebook and opened it and creased the pages backwards. He produced a pencil from his pocket, licked its point, and began to write in the notebook.

'The plague cart?' he asked. 'Is that another name for an ambulance?'

'You could call it that,' Adam said. He brought his hands together, so that all the tips of the fingers were touching each other. He then locked his joined hands underneath his chin.

'Could you tell me anything about John Purefoy? He used to make sausage-skins, didn't he?' The cub looked round the room. 'Funny taste in knick-knacks. Phoney as hell.'

'No,' Adam said. 'He never made sausage-skins. And everything in here is genuine.'

'Noyes said he made sausage-skins.'

'Noyes is wrong. Noyes is always wrong. That is the only thing you need to know as a reporter.' Adam paused. 'Enough of this question and answer game. I will dictate to you the obituary of the Raker.'

'The Raker?'

The cub sat on the sofa with his pencil ready. Adam ignored his question.

'John Purefoy,' Adam said slowly, 'called the Raker, died by his own choice last night. He was born to die. He was one of the few who always lived with his death. He was a rich man, but poor in what we need to allow ourselves to survive, poor in the power of forgetting. He thought of everyone, because he understood the pain of his own humanity. He gave himself to everyone, because he suffered truly in himself. He did little so as not to increase the pain in the world. Because of his infinite generosity, he would admit to no kindness. He lived strictly by his words. He was an honest man, and the last gentleman.'

Adam stopped speaking. The cub had given up writing, and was looking at Adam in amazement.

'They'll never print that,' he said.

Adam spoke finally.

'Go,' he said. 'Go.'

'My assignment . . .'

'For God's sake, go.'

The reporter rose and went out of the room. Adam watched his neck pink under his idiotic curls, his buttocks still puffed out with puppy-fat and hope. Hope. Wasn't that the greatest evil of all, hope, the delusion that Pandora had let out of her box with all the plagues of mankind to keep human beings from general suicide?

Adam looked once more round the Raker's room, from the chimney-piece with its five *memento moris*, past the pictures on the wall in praise of death or still-lives, past the grey silk hangings, past the copies of Egyptian and Etruscan mummies, to where the Raker had stood by his real poisons, with the hand plunged within the jar, marked HEMLOCK. The shelf was now empty. The Raker was gone. All the objects now belonged to Adam. They would clutter his bare room, his monk's cell. They would stand on the floor and lie on the bed. He would stumble over death, sit by death, work beside death, sleep with death only a hand's breadth away. Death would become his familiar. He would always wake in the plague pit, with the touch and the smell of the dead about him. With his rake, he would tidy the sweepings from the houses of the dead, so that others could bear to live in those houses in their own sweet human ignorance.

Adam walked over to the Raker's desk. A sheet of paper was lying there. He sat in the Raker's chair and took out his own pen. He wrote, after some thought:

QUINCE, Adam.
He worked for twelve years, and did nothing.
He lived a full life, and remained empty.
He was born for the first time at the age of thirty, and he
died on the same day for the rest of his life.

ALSO AVAILABLE FROM VALANCOURT BOOKS

Lightning Source UK Ltd.
Milton Keynes UK
UKOW04f0910301013

220053UK00002B/22/P